# STICKLER
## and ME

# STICKLER and ME

### by MORLEY TORGOV

RAINCOAST BOOKS

*Vancouver*

*Raincoast Books gratefully acknowledges the ongoing support of the Canada Council for the Arts; the British Columbia Arts Council; and the Government of Canada through the Department of Canadian Heritage Book Publishing Industry Development Program (BPIDP).*

For their encouragement, advice and assistance, my thanks to Beverley Slopen, Lynn Henry, Joy Gugeler, Joanne DeLio, Marvin Cohen, Henry Campbell, Anna Pisani and, of course, Anna Pearl.

Cover art by Greg Banning
Cover design by Ingrid Paulson
Typeset by Ben Blackstock

National Library of Canada Cataloguing in Publication Data
Torgov, Morley, 1927-
  Stickler and me

ISBN 1-55192-546-X

I. Title.
PS8589.O675S74 2002        C813'.54        C2001-911659-4
PR9199.3.T613S74 2002

Raincoast Books
9050 Shaughnessy Street
Vancouver, British Columbia
Canada, V6P 6E5
www.raincoast.com

Printed and bound in Canada by Webcom.

1 2 3 4 5 6 7 8 9 10

For Benjamin, Sydney, Allison,
Rebecca and Marshall

# **Prologue**

et's say I'm strolling along a beach somewhere. Suddenly I stub my big toe against something hard that's stuck in the sand — a bottle that has obviously drifted ashore. I pick it up because, who knows, maybe there's an urgent message inside. I manage to extract the cork and out pops a genie. Grateful to be released, the genie says to me, "Benjamin Marshall, you are now fourteen years of age and therefore old enough to know what you want most in life. Ask, and it shall be granted."

The truth? I wouldn't have a clue how to answer. I still haven't figured out what I want most in my life.

But I will tell you this: If the genie asked what I did *not* want most, I could give my reply in less time than it takes to say "Ben" (which is what I prefer to be called).

What I would *not* want most is to be able to see into the future. Futures, I've learned, are dangerous things ... full of people you're not sure you want to encounter, things you never expected to hear, corners you never expected to turn and — above all — trouble, serious trouble, you never expected to get into.

How have I come to know this? Because about this time one year ago, when I was thirteen, I made a decision about how I wanted to spend July and August of that summer. Without realizing what I was getting into, I opened a curtain, stepped onto a strange stage and found myself right in the middle of …

Well, it's taken all these months to record what I saw and managed to piece together from the recollections of other people involved one way or another.

Where to begin? Like all stories, this one begins with a question.

# One

"**Y**ou're sure about this, Ben? I mean, it's not too late to change your mind, y'know."

My mother was standing in the doorway of my bedroom, arms folded, watching me squeeze, push, twist and jam the last item on my list — a pair of sneakers that smelled like a gymnasium — into an already crammed duffel bag.

I pretended I hadn't heard her question. "My sweatshirt," I said, remembering it was nowhere to be seen, "you didn't put it in the laundry, I hope?"

"Which sweatshirt?" My mother's face was all innocence. I could tell she was playing dumb.

I said, rolling my eyes, my tone of voice menacing, "C'mon, Mom, you know which sweatshirt. Where'd you stash it away?"

It took a split second for her expression to change to bossy. "You are *not* taking that sweatshirt to Port Sanford, Ben. I absolutely forbid you to wear that rag outside of this room. Your grandfather will be nothing short of mortified if you show up on his doorstep with that tasteless, disgusting, insulting — "

"Okay, okay," I said quickly, raising my hand in a gesture of peace. "I didn't think Gramps was so darn sensitive."

"That's right, Ben, you didn't *think*."

I wasn't ready to give up totally without an argument on the subject. "I still don't see what's so tasteless, disgusting and insulting. All it's got printed across the chest is FIRST THING, LET'S KILL ALL THE LAWYERS. I think Shakespeare said it in one of his plays. It's funny. Besides, I didn't buy the sweatshirt, Dad did."

"Which is the second reason why you're not to take it with you."

"The first reason being what?"

"The first reason being that my father ... your grandfather ... is very proud of the fact that he's been practising law for nearly fifty years. He would definitely not find your sweatshirt the least bit amusing."

I said, "What would bother Gramps more, the idea of killing all the lawyers, or the idea that Dad bought me the sweatshirt?"

"Take your pick," my mother replied.

It was no secret, at least no secret in our immediate family, how much my grandfather and his son-in-law disliked one another. My physics teacher would have explained it as a simple example of two substances with similar inherent properties repelling each other — a fancy scientific term for two men with one thing in common: each one was positive he and he alone had all the right answers to all the questions in the world.

My parents' divorce a little over a year ago, just before my twelfth birthday, certainly did nothing to smooth out the relationship between my grandfather, Ira Lamport, and my father, Talbot Marshall, whom Gramps referred to always with a slight sneer as "my son-in-law, the great surgeon." Naturally Grandfather took Mom's side; after all, she *is* his daughter.

"Is Gramps still in a lousy mood?" I asked. "I mean, about the divorce and all?"

"Your grandfather is a proud, stubborn and lonely man, Ben. He's been that way for a long time. Our marriage, your father's and mine, was one rock in his path, our splitting up was another. Honestly, I can't guarantee that spending the summer with him up in Port Sanford is going to be a bowl of cherries. Not for you, not for him. That's why I repeat: Are you sure you don't want to change your mind and take advantage of our offer?"

"*Our* offer? — "

"Your father and I agreed that we'd share the cost if you preferred to spend July and part of August down east at Camp Pinestone. That way, if he's not tied up at the hospital, your father can spend some time with you on visitors' days."

Without any enthusiasm, I said, "That'd sure be a big thrill."

"And when I get back from doing my research in France you and I could maybe hop in the car and take a trip down to the States ... Lake Placid, the Adirondacks ... something like that."

"You're forgetting something, aren't you?" I said.

Mother frowned. "Forgetting? What?"

"That I got kicked out of Camp Pinestone last summer. I wasn't even there a whole week."

"That's all in the past, Ben. We have to learn to put things like that behind us and get on with our lives, just as your father and I are doing."

My mother's advice didn't sound too convincing. "One cigarette ... one crummy itty-bitty cigarette ... the first time in my whole life I ever smoked ... and ol' Sourpuss Macklin says to me 'Marshall, that's a nicotine stain on your finger and a stain on your record; there's no room here for kids who disobey the rules.' And out I went."

Giving me one of her patient smiles, my mother said, "Well, Ben, the good news is, you're a year older and a year wiser now, and Mr. Macklin assures me you'd be welcome."

"You mean," I said, "the huge amount of money you'd have

to pay to send me to Camp Pinestone would be welcome."

My mother shook her head sadly. "I don't know how, when or why you became such a cynic, Ben."

"The answer's easy," I said. "Just watching you and Dad in action day after day, month after month, these last coupla years would be enough to make any kid think the human race was a big mistake."

"And I suppose, Mr. Cynic, you imagine the next six or seven weeks with your grandfather will improve your outlook on the world?"

"Anything's better," I said, "than having to jump into an ice-cold lake at seven in the morning, or slogging through a swamp with a stupid canoe and backpack on my shoulders and mosquitoes up my shorts."

My mother gave a deep sigh. "Some of the happiest days of my life were spent camping when I was your age, Ben. I loved the canoe trips, the clean air and clean water, being so close to nature."

"Yeah, well, how come," I said, "we never got a cottage like a lot of other people?"

"Because your father simply didn't have the time. Summer weekends were often the busiest times for an orthopedic surgeon. Still are, in fact. You know … car accidents, boating accidents, things like that."

"Plus," I said, "the fact that you were always getting last-minute calls from your boss at the *Gazette*. Remember? 'Allison, you gotta go here, Allison, you gotta go there.' Always it was rush, rush. So it wasn't Dad's fault all the time."

"Well, Ben," my mother said, sounding resigned, "since you've made up your mind that getting to know your grandfather is preferable to communing with nature, you'd better take careful note of some important do's and don'ts about being under the same roof with Ira Lamport."

I pretended to reach for a note pad on my desk. "Should I be writing down these tips, Mom?"

"Don't be a smart alec," she said. "Just listen ... for a change."

"I'm all ears," I said, trying to look serious.

"All right. Now listen carefully, Ben. You've always made a point of plugging your nose whenever he lights up one of his big cigars. Refrain from doing that from now on. At your grandfather's age he's going to smoke cigars whether or not you approve. Understood?"

I nodded yes. "What else?"

"He allows himself to say the word 'damn'. Otherwise he frowns on foul language. I know that you and your friends have a whole warehouse full of four-letter words at your command, Ben. For the next six weeks or so, let not a single obscenity be uttered from your lips, certainly never in his presence. Is *that* understood?"

Again I nodded.

"Tip number three: He's not a believer in ostentatious living — "

"In *what*? — "

"Let me put it another way, Ben. Your grandfather's not a big spender. Never was, never will be. So, no wisecracks from you about his clothes, his car, his office furniture, the house. It's been some years since you were up in Port Sanford, and you're going to find that nothing has changed. Take things as you find them and try to make the best of it."

I was beginning to wonder whether my choices for how I was to spend the summer consisted of two evils. Maybe Camp Pinestone was the lesser of two evils, after all. My mother seemed to sense the doubt that was growing inside me. "Want me to continue?" she asked.

"It's beginning to sound like I'm going to reform school," I said.

"Which brings up the most important point of all about your grandfather, Ben. He likes things done his way, and laws are like a religion to him. They are not to be broken ... under *any* circumstances."

"Does he know ... I mean, about me being kicked out of camp last summer?"

"No. We told him you had to come home early because you were allergic to the dampness and moulds in the cabins. The point is, he plays everything straight ... strictly by the books. You get the message?"

I stared down at the duffel bag lying at my feet. It was still open, its strings as limp as pieces of spaghetti. In my mind I had a vision of a man I didn't get to see often and really didn't know well, and a vague recollection of a town I hadn't visited in something like three or four years. There was still time to unpack, to make other arrangements.

Smiling wisely, my mother said, "You're having second thoughts, aren't you, Ben?"

My mother's description of my grandfather came back to me right then: "*a proud, stubborn and lonely man.*" Was it possible that pride and stubbornness could be handed down from grandfather to grandson like, say, a gold watch or a chess set or a shelf full of old encyclopedias?

Pride wasn't out of the question, to be honest. I remember one morning, two years ago, my first morning in Grade Seven after summer holiday. Our new teacher, Mr. Abernethy, was doing roll call. One by one he said, "And what's your name? And who are your parents and what do they do? And do you have grandparents? And what do *they* do?" I said that my mom was a journalist and my dad was a doctor. Not an ordinary doctor, I said, but a surgeon. Then I told Abernethy my grandfather was a lawyer, the kind that goes to court. "Well, well, Mister Ben Marshall, you're following in big footsteps!" says Abernethy. For the rest of the term I was called "Mister Ben Marshall." It was a joke, sort of. But secretly I was proud.

And stubborn? Oh, I could be stubborn, all right. "You're more than just stubborn, Ben," my mother would say, "you're downright obstinate." Usually she'd say this during an argument about my taste in music or literature or art. I was into comic books, but my mom and dad — can you believe this? — thought I should be reading the classics — Mark Twain, Dickens, Shakespeare. Shakespeare! Naturally I said no. That's when I got the stubborn speech. I'm not sure why, but I began to take it as a compliment.

Maybe it was pride. Maybe I was simply being stubborn. More likely it was a bit of both. "Yes," I said, "I *am* having second thoughts, but I'm still going to Port Sanford."

But as I reached down to tie the strings of the duffel bag, I realized that there was a third reason — the most important reason of all at the moment — why I'd made up my mind to go. Like Gramps, I was lonely.

There are lots of things that can happen to a kid my age: sickness, handicaps, homelessness, hunger, but feeling lonely is the worst, take my word for it. And it has nothing to do with the number of people around you. I haven't figured out why, exactly. All I know is, what goes on outside a person is one thing; what goes on *inside* is another. Sometimes one has very little to do with the other.

I checked the time on my wristwatch. "We better get going, Mom," I said. "The bus leaves for Port Sanford in half an hour."

It was early July 1962, and that morning, at the newsstand

in the bus terminal downtown, President John Kennedy's promise was splashed in giant headlines across the front pages of the morning papers: American astronauts would be the first humans to land on the moon.

Back in January of last year, I'd watched on television as Kennedy was sworn in as president of the United States. One line in his speech came back to me now: "Ask not what your country can do for you — ask what you can do for your country." I figured nobody could do more for his country than climb inside a rocket and fly to the moon. Dad, when I told him this, looked at me as if I was out of my mind. And Mom said, "Ben, never, *never* take anything a politician says too seriously."

I took my seat on the bus with only moments to spare, sat back and watched Toronto begin to disappear, saw the long open highway come into view ahead of us. And all the way, I felt as though *I* was the one making the first trip to the moon. Not the bright side, the side you see. I was going to the far side, the dark part, the part I hardly knew anything about.

# Two

I made my first big mistake during a conversation that took place over dinner the day I arrived at Port Sanford.

Grandfather Lamport, despite the fact that he was going on seventy-five years of age, was a very busy man. He was the oldest lawyer in the Port Sanford area, having opened his law practice in the town soon after receiving his call to the bar almost a half-century earlier. Many of his clients were about the same age. They were very loyal to him, and he was very loyal to them. "I'm like an old pair of shoes," he said to me, "and they feel comfortable with me and trust my advice. Maybe some day, Ben, you'll become a lawyer, set up your law office right here in Port Sanford. It's a good life, you know. Come to think of it, how'd you like to take over my practice when you're old enough?"

"I wouldn't," I said.

Gramps frowned. "Wouldn't?"

"No," I said. "I'd rather be an airline pilot and fly all over the world instead of being stuck — " The look on my grandfather's face told me I'd better not finish what I was going to say.

"An airline pilot, eh?" Gramps said, punctuating the remark with a snort. "Not much of a life, far as I can tell. Pilots have to retire when they reach their fifties. Lawyers, on the other hand, *never* have to retire because of their age. We can live a purposeful life right up to the day we're too old to get out of bed, thank God. Look at me, for instance." There was an unmistakable note of pride in his voice.

I studied my grandfather for a moment. He was tall but beginning to stoop a bit around the shoulders now. He still possessed a full head of hair, but it was snow-white. The wrinkles in his forehead, around his eyes and down the sides of his cheeks reminded me of furrows you see in fields that have just been plowed. I noticed, too, that he seldom smiled and whenever he did he seemed to be holding back, as though he was afraid to overdo it. His clothes, unlike my father's, looked like pictures I'd seen in old department store catalogues. Every day he wore the same polka-dot bow tie, which he tied himself. His suits were made of some kind of tweedy material, the jackets baggy at the elbows, the trousers baggy at the knees. For as long as I could recall, Gramps always had a wintry look, even when the temperature outdoors sent birds scurrying into the trees seeking shade.

At this point I made my second big mistake. I said, looking Gramps straight in the eye, "I don't think I'd care to be working when I'm as old as you are. What I mean is — "

"I know what you mean," Grandfather cut in, looking displeased. "No explanation's required. Well, young fella, I'll say this much for you: at least you say what's on your mind. Not that saying what's on your mind is always a virtue." And with that, my grandfather hid himself behind that week's edition of the *Port Sanford Echo*.

If two mistakes are bad, is a third mistake necessarily worse?

I'm afraid so.

I had brought along one of my most prized possessions, a

portable combination radio and record player, and a dozen or so of my favourite records. Now, there's only one thing more boring than packing before you go on a trip, and that's *un*packing after you get to wherever you're going. So to relieve the boredom of extracting all the personal belongings I'd stuffed into my duffel bag (which, I imagined, was something like what a dentist experiences when he's pulling teeth) I first plugged my radio/record player into an extension cord connected to the only wall socket I could find, one near the bed I was to occupy. The socket was already putting out more than its fair share of electricity, with two extension cords leading from it, one servicing two bedside reading lamps, the other servicing an old-fashioned fan that seemed to do nothing but rearrange the warm air in the room. Still, I figured one more appliance added to the load wouldn't matter. After all, from what I'd seen of Grandfather's house since my arrival before dinner, it looked like one of those fortresses built to last a thousand years, with electrical wiring to match.

I flipped through my records. Yes, I'd remembered to pick the ones I liked best: "Rock Around the Clock" featuring Bill Haley and the Comets; a couple of hits by Elvis Presley, a couple more by Little Richard; "Let's Twist Again" by Chubby Checker.

Then I came to the newest item in my collection, songs by a guy who sounded at times as though he was singing through his nose and other times as if he was growling from somewhere down a deep mineshaft. In between, he was strumming his guitar while at the same time making foghorn noises with his harmonica.

But it was his words that I couldn't seem to get enough of, and I had been playing this record over and over at home until I'd managed to memorize them. I could even belt out the lyrics at the top of my lungs, syllable by syllable, with the same twanging and rasping sounds as the singer himself made.

The guy's name was Bob Dylan. He was only a little over twenty years old — not that much older than me, come to think of it — and I had the feeling that when he wrote his songs he was reading my mind. In his eyes, the world was beginning to look upside down. There was this craziness going on that people called "The Cold War" between the Russians and the Americans. Everywhere there was talk that Russia and the United States were locked in a fight to the death over whether Communism would be allowed to spread all over the world. Atomic bombs were being tested. There was a good chance that the human race was going to blow itself to bits and life on earth would cease to exist except for a few freaks who might survive. Meanwhile at school we were into a new and very different kind of "fire" drill. Instead of dashing for the nearest exit, the trick when the alarm sounded was to dive under your desk, cover your face and hope to God you were still alive and in one piece when it was all over. The problem was, our teachers weren't talking about an ordinary fire; they were talking about an atomic blast, like the one that turned Hiroshima into four square miles of rubble near the end of the Second World War. Talk about nightmares! Every time we saw pictures of Hiroshima or had one of these drills, I didn't have a good night's sleep for a week after.

As far as Bob Dylan was concerned, the older generations — our fathers and mothers and grandfathers and grandmothers — were making a terrible mess of things. Spending fortunes on guns instead of feeding the poor. Worrying about death instead of looking for better ways to live. Hating instead of loving. Making rules and regulations instead of enjoying freedom.

As far as *I* was concerned, you didn't have to look far to see how right Bob Dylan was. All you had to do was look at my own parents. Spending money — tons of it — on lawyers to get their divorce. Arguing for hours over whether this silver platter or that crystal vase belonged to him or to her. Hating instead of loving. And having the nerve to make rules and regulations about *my* life when, all the time, it seemed to me that they had no idea how to rule and regulate their own lives.

So I put on my Dylan record. Full volume. And I began to sing, also at full volume. The sound boomed and crackled out of my record player like thunder and lightning.

Soon the bed lamps began to flicker. So did the ceiling light fixture. The fan, droning on, slowed suddenly, then picked up, then slowed again. Plaster walls that had never before heard such noises might crack under the pressure, for all I knew. But who cared?

This was the music, these were the words and the thoughts of my new hero, Bob Dylan.

And then came the unexpected pounding on the door of my room. And before I could reply the door was flung open and Grandfather was standing there. For a moment he was speechless. Just stood there like some tall granite statue, filling the dark oak frame of the doorway. But it quickly turned out that the "statue" had a voice and lungs every bit as powerful as Bob Dylan's.

"Turn that damn racket off!" Grandfather shouted.

I couldn't believe that anybody would regard the singing of my hero as a "damn racket." "But that's Bob Dylan, Gramps," I pleaded.

"I don't give a damn if it's God and Satan rolled into one. Turn it off this instant!"

My mother had warned me about using foul language in the old man's presence, but I figured if *he* was allowed to use "damn" freely … well, what was good for the goose was good for the gander, as the old saying goes. "Dylan writes the best damn songs in the world," I said, making no move to shut off the record player.

"'Damn' is not a word that's permitted in this house, young man," Grandfather said, still shouting.

I began to protest. "Then how come — "

But my grandfather was not listening. "You kids listen to this kind of trash and your minds turn to trash."

"Maybe it would do people like you a lot of good to listen once in a while."

"Listen to what? Some cranky little rock-and-roller who thinks he's got the answers to the world's problems?"

Without another word, Grandfather moved toward the record player, intending to shut it off, but I stood rooted in front of the machine, blocking his way.

Seeing this, my grandfather, with surprising swiftness, changed direction and managed to get hold of the extension cord, which he yanked out of the wall socket with a single powerful sweep of his right arm. The cord flew out of the socket, bringing with it a shower of sparks. A split second later, Grandfather and I stood in total darkness. Through the open doorway of my room, I could see that every light in the house had gone out. In fact, everything else in the house that owed its life to electricity had suddenly stopped breathing — the refrigerator, the lamps, the television, the radio — everything except the telephone, which Grandfather used to summon an electrician.

It was almost midnight when Charley Henry, the electrician, wiped his hands on his overalls, pulled the pencil from behind his ear and did some quick arithmetic on a slip of paper.

"That'll be two hundred and eighty-seven, seventy-two, Ira," said Charley Henry, "including parts and labour."

I watched my grandfather write the cheque. Each letter, each number, seemed to take him forever. It seemed to take forever, too, to screw the top back on his old-fashioned fountain pen afterward. I had the feeling that Grandfather had just parted with his last cent.

"Sorry about this, Ira," Charley Henry said, taking the cheque, "I guess it's an expensive lesson, eh?" The electrician was kneeling, placing his tools in a weather-beaten wooden toolbox. He looked up at my grandfather and chuckled. "Strikes me that an old timer like you woulda known better than to yank an electric cord out of a socket like that, Ira. Oh, well, nobody's perfect."

When he said "Nobody's perfect," Charley Henry gave me a wink and a wry grin. I shot a quick glance at my grandfather. The old man, as the look on his face made very clear, was *not* amused.

We went to bed that night, Gramps and I, without exchanging another word.

And that was how it passed … Day One in the house of Ira Lamport up in Port Sanford.

Gramps lived alone in a large three-storey brick house in the centre of Port Sanford (my grandmother had died when I was a baby). His law office took up the large front room on the ground floor of the house, the one that served as the parlour where he and my grandmother used to entertain company when they were younger. Every morning Miss Trimble, Gramps' secretary, would arrive and the two of them would close the heavy sliding oak doors that separated the office from the other rooms. For hours afterward all I could hear was my grandfather's muffled voice as he gave dictation, or Miss Trimble rattling away at the antiquated typewriter on her desk, which was across the room from his. There were stacks of files and loose papers all over the place, and several tall bookcases with thick volumes that contained all the laws in the world, or so I imagined.

Unlike Grandfather's office, which was cluttered from floor to ceiling and wall to wall, the other rooms in the old house were barren. There were no nooks and crannies, no windowless holes-in-the-wall where a child's imagination could conjure up secrets and mysteries. Apart from a handful of faded family photographs on the fireplace mantel in the dining room, and the odd wishy-washy painting of a country landscape here and there, the house was as grim as a late November day. The only truly bright and colourful feature was a pastel portrait of my grandmother that hung in Grandfather's bedroom, set so as to catch the sunlight that streamed in through a bay window. I had the feeling that when she died, much of that house died with her.

As far as I could tell, there were no kids my age, or even close to my age, in that neighbourhood. I'd brought my bicycle with me, and in my explorations around the town it seemed to me that most of the local citizens my parents' age lived on the outskirts or in the surrounding countryside. The folks in the vicinity of Gramps' house for the most part were well on in years and regarded me as a nuisance whenever I whizzed up and down the street on my bike, releasing my stored-up energy.

I was beginning to think that this summer in Port Sanford would never end. I resented my mother for being away, somewhere off in Europe. She might as well have been on another planet, maybe Mars or the moon, as far as I was concerned. As for my father, it was plain to me that his favourite spot on earth was an operating room, and that his medical instruments were closer to him than I was.

And as for my grandfather, well, we simply didn't seem to have a whole lot to say to one another.

One day, toward the end of the first week, Gramps and I were having lunch, thick roast beef sandwiches that his house-keeper Mrs. Bjorklund had made (I'll say *one* thing about living with grandfather: his housekeeper was a far better cook than my mother's). We were interrupted by Miss Trimble, who looked anxious. "Mr. Lamport," she said in that timid voice of hers, "I hate to spoil your lunch but Mrs. O'Hearn is on the phone. It's the same as always, I'm afraid — "

"And I suppose the sky's falling as usual?" Gramps said, putting down his sandwich.

Miss Trimble lowered her voice to a whisper. "She wants to change her will."

Gramps exploded. "Good heavens, not again! Doesn't that woman have anything better to do?"

Now Miss Trimble's voice became a squeak. "She says she's dying."

My grandfather groaned. I could tell that he was having difficulty remaining patient. "She says the same thing every time she calls."

"I think it's different this time," said the secretary. "The doctor's at her house, and I understand some of her relatives have gathered at her bedside."

"Very well," Grandfather said, finishing his iced tea in a single gulp. He turned to me. "Ben, I know it's been boring for you, being 'stuck' as you put it, here in this house. I want you to come with me to Mrs. O'Hearn's place. It's about thirty miles out of town, a big estate, maybe fifty, sixty acres or there-abouts. Farm animals, prize livestock, barns and stables so immaculate you can eat off the floors. It'll be a learning experience for you, young man. Might even change your mind about spending the better part of your life up in the air, show you the wisdom of staying down on the ground where the good Lord intended mankind to be."

I have to admit I went along not because I gave a hoot about estates and farm animals and eating off barn floors, but because I wanted a change of scenery, *any* change.

Climbing into the front passenger seat of my grandfather's ten-year-old Buick, I asked, "This Mrs. O'Hearn, does she have any kids out there on her estate ... I mean, any kids my age?"

Gramps looked at me as if I'd just said something stupid. "Good God, no," he replied, "the woman's ninety years old. Never had any children, as a matter of fact. She's what you call a dowager."

I looked puzzled. "What's a dowager?"

Gramps looked straight ahead as he stepped on the gas. All he said was, "You'll soon find out."

The farm known as "O'Hearn Estate " was a good half-hour drive from Port Sanford. We drove in silence, Gramps keeping a sharp lookout along the stretch of two-lane highway, muttering constantly about the damn gravel trucks and eighteen-wheel transports that hogged the road and rumbled past us at speeds much above the limits posted on the road signs. The countryside was an uninterrupted series of rolling silvery-green hills, guarded here and there by regiments of trees recently planted that stood in perfect rows like soldiers. On either side of the highway, set well back, stood splendid country houses, their brick or stone walls old but dignified, their wooden porches and windowsills and doorways glistening as though painted that very day. I figured the people who lived in these houses weren't the kind of farmers you saw in movies, bending over to pick potatoes or cotton from dawn to dusk, heading into town in beat-up jalopies to buy supplies at the general store with empty pockets and empty promises to pay once they'd managed to sell their crops. No, the folks inhabiting these farm properties had to be prosperous, the sort of folks who never worried about where their next meal was coming from, and who displayed their family names on fancy signs fixed to their gateposts.

"The people who live out here, are they your clients?" I asked Grandfather at last.

"Most of 'em," Gramps said. "We've grown up together and grown old together."

I thought about my grandfather and his clients for a moment, then said, "There's something I don't understand about why you're going to visit this Mrs. O'Hearn — "

"What don't you understand?"

"Well, if the old lady's dying, like Miss Trimble said, how come she wants to see her *lawyer*? You'd think she'd really want to see her doctor."

"Answer's simple," Grandfather said, glancing at me, then returning his eyes to the road ahead. "Doctor can't do beans for her now. She's ninety years of age, like an old battery that can't take a charge. Me? I can give 'er something a doctor can't — peace of mind."

"Is that what a will is all about, peace of mind?" I asked.

"Yes, you might put it that way. A will's a very important document that a person signs that says what's to happen to that person's worldly possessions. After all, Ben, most people work hard to accumulate things ... property, furniture, equipment, a business, money. A person has the right to say who should manage these things when he or she passes on, who should be the beneficiaries, the people entitled to the benefits of whatever's left behind. Sometimes, like the case of Mrs.

O'Hearn, what's left behind is extremely valuable, and she wants to make sure things are done exactly the way *she* wants them to be done, after she's gone."

I hesitated to ask more questions, partly because Gramps was becoming increasingly irritated about the traffic on the highway, but more, I guess, because up to this point he and I hadn't made a habit of engaging in lengthy conversations, especially about his professional activities. Still my curiosity about Mrs. O'Hearn would not rest. "Gramps," I said, watching the expression on his face for any sign that I was disturbing his concentration, "there's something else I don't understand. Back at the house, when Miss Trimble told you there was a call from Mrs. O'Hearn, why did you look so ... so fed up?"

For the first time since we'd gotten into the Buick, a slight smile crept across Gramps' face. "You don't miss a trick, do you, young fella? All right, then, I'll tell you why. Mrs. O'Hearn, like I said before, is a dowager. A dowager is a widow whose husband has died and left her so rich she couldn't get around to spending all that money if she lived to be a hundred and eighty!"

"Well, what's so bad about that?"

"Nothing's bad about being rich, *sometimes*. But in Mrs. O'Hearn's case, she and her husband never had any children. So she's devoted a lot of her time to some local charities. Plus she's got these three close relatives, two nephews and a niece. Three good-for-nothings, if you ask me. All they do, the nephews and niece, is hang around like buzzards ... waiting for the old lady to die, waiting to get their greedy mitts on as much of her fortune as they can. Dollars to donuts the three of 'em will be glued to her bedside when we get there, hovering over her, pretending their own lives are coming to an end, weeping false tears into their handkerchiefs."

"You really don't think much of them, do you, Gramps?"

This brought the first hearty laugh from my grandfather that I'd heard since the day I arrived at Port Sanford. "That's the understatement of the century," Gramps said. "Truth is, I loathe the sight of that trio of sloths. Never done a decent day's work in their miserable little lives, not a single one of 'em."

"So that's the reason you're fed up?" I asked.

"Not really, Ben. After all, they're *her* relatives, not mine, thank God. I'm just fed up because every time I think we're done with her will, she ups and changes her mind about something or other, and we almost have to start from scratch. No sooner does the old lady sign one will than she's on the phone telling me she wants to change this or change that. One day she decides to leave her string of cultured pearls to Priscilla Cranbrooke ... that's her niece ... next day she's decided instead that she wants the pearls sold and the money given to the local branch of the Sally Ann — "

"The Sally Ann? — "

"Salvation Army to you. It's enough to drive any lawyer crazy. Crazy while she's alive. Maybe crazier after she's died."

"Why after she's died?" I wanted to know. "Once she's dead she can't make any more changes, can she?"

This brought a second laugh from Gramps. "Don't be too sure, Ben," he said. "Rebecca O'Hearn's the kind of person who could still be telling me what to do, giving me orders in that regal manner of hers, long after she's dead." Then Grandfather added with a chuckle, "Long after *I'm* dead too, for that matter."

There were so many things I didn't understand. One question seemed to lead to another and another. "I don't get it, Gramps. Once Mrs. O'Hearn has passed away, isn't that the end as far as you're concerned?"

"Good grief, no!" Gramps said. "Every will has to have at least one person who's appointed to manage the deceased's affairs. That person's called an executor and trustee. In the case of Mrs. O'Hearn's estate, she's appointed me her sole executor and trustee."

"You mean, you're responsible alone to see to it that all the things she's said in her will — "

"All her instructions, yes — "

" — all those things get done?"

"Correct. That's my job, to carry out her instructions to the letter exactly as she directed. No ifs, ands or buts."

"Is that why you're called 'trustee,' because people trust you?"

"I like to think so, Ben. Besides, a lawyer in a town like Port Sanford can make a pretty comfortable living because folks in these parts trust his knowledge, his integrity, his experience."

I thought for a moment about this, then said, "Same as airline pilots. Passengers trust *them* too, for the same reasons, I guess."

Gramps chose to ignore this comparison. He pointed to a long stretch of freshly painted white fences lining one side of the roadway now. "O'Hearn Estate," he announced. "We're here. Brace yourself, young fella. You ever meet a dying person before?"

"No."

"Well, here's your first opportunity," Gramps said, swinging the Buick hard right between the fieldstone gates with the polished brass signs that read "O'Hearn." "Death and dying are as much part of life as eating and sleeping and getting up and going to work, Ben. You might as well find that out now as later. Let's call it part of your education."

I wasn't sure I agreed with Grandfather. The prospect of catching even a quick glimpse of this old lady, this Rebecca O'Hearn, didn't appeal to me one bit. I'd seen people dying in movies and on television. That was educational enough for me.

As Gramps pulled the car into the circular part of the drive-way in front of the main house, we noticed that there were four or five cars parked ahead of us. "Looks like they're here already, the buzzards," Gramps said, looking as though he'd just tasted something sour. "And that black two-door, that's undoubtedly Father Hussey, the old lady's priest. Well, maybe she's not fooling this time. Maybe she's really on her way. Come along, Ben. I guess there's not a moment to waste, after all."

I hung back in the passenger seat as Gramps got out of the car. "Come along, young fella," Gramps called, coming around the front of the car and over to my side.

"Do I have to?"

My grandfather didn't bother to reply. He simply opened the front door on my side of the Buick and stood there, in the driveway, with a stern expression on his face that told me I had no choice.

# Three

We had barely mounted the broad flagstone front steps of the O'Hearn house (mansion was more like it) when the door opened and a large woman called out, "Thank heaven you're here at last, Mr. Lamport. She's been driving us all right up the wall today."

"She's up to her old tricks again, eh?" my grandfather said as we were let into the large high-ceilinged foyer. He turned to me. "Ben, I want you to meet Mrs. Tidy, Hilda Tidy. Hilda here's in charge of the house and her husband Bill's in charge of the other buildings on the property. Folks around here refer to them, to him and her that is, as Neat 'n Tidy. Look around, Ben, you'll understand why."

Hilda Tidy beamed. "Oh, go on with you, you old flatterer," she said to my grandfather. To me she said, "And you must be Mr. Lamport's grandson, the one who's spending the summer here in Port Sanford. Now don't bother asking how I know that. In these parts everybody knows everything that's going on. I just baked some shortbread cookies. Mrs. O'Hearn's favourite, don't you know. Would you like some?"

I was about to accept Mrs. Tidy's offer when my grandfather stepped between us. "First I want to introduce him to the lady of the house upstairs, then I'll send him back down to the kitchen for cookies." Reluctantly I began to follow Gramps, trailing after him as he laboriously made his way up a long flight of circular steps that led to the second storey. At the top of the stairs he paused. I wasn't certain whether he was catching his breath or preparing himself for the unpleasant task of facing his client and dealing with her dying wishes.

Straightening his back, as though gathering up courage, he strode down the long hallway. Its walls were covered with oil paintings, mostly family portraits, I assumed, though some of the pictures were of racehorses. Mrs. O'Hearn's bedroom was at the far end of the hallway, behind a set of doors that had been left wide apart to permit a slight breeze from the open windows to circulate.

The first thing that caught my eye was an enormous mahogany four-poster bed, supported on legs thick as those of an elephant. It was the kind of bed, I reckoned, that would be left standing without so much as a scratch if the place were struck by a tornado. In the broad expanse of blankets topped by an ornate quilt, the occupant of the bed looked almost lost. All I could see was this small face, pale, surprisingly unwrinkled considering Mrs. O'Hearn's age, the head propped up on overstuffed pillows. The rest of her — her body and limbs — was concealed under all those bedcovers, which struck me as odd bearing in mind the July heat. I supposed that being old and being cold went hand in hand.

There were four visitors already in the room as we entered, two men, a woman, and a third man in a black suit with one of those white collars that priests and ministers wear, who I took to be Father Hussey. None of them bothered to greet Grandfather and me, and I assumed that this was how people were supposed to conduct themselves in the presence of someone who was about to die. The woman, who looked about the same age as my mother, was clutching some tissues and her eyes were red-rimmed as she stared down at the old lady buried under the blankets and quilt. I heard her say, as though talking to herself, "I hope she's warm enough," but the others didn't seem to share her concern. The two men, who were roughly my father's age, also stood looking down at Mrs. O'Hearn, but showed no emotion. These three were on Mrs. O'Hearn's left. On her right side stood Father Hussey, slipping a narrow prayer shawl around his neck, then opening a small wooden box from which he extracted a bottle of some kind of liquid. The woman, the one clutching the tissues, broke into a soft sob. One of the men behind her spoke up sharply, "Priscilla, get hold of yourself!" This only forced a louder sob from the woman, and the man who'd spoken so gruffly turned away, looking disgusted.

The priest began to say something that sounded like Latin as he unscrewed the top of the bottle. Just as he began to speak, I heard a low growl. At first it seemed to be coming from the hallway outside, but as it grew louder and more ominous I realized that it was coming from some place very close to where my grandfather and I were standing, which was near the foot of the bed.

Suddenly, Mrs. O'Hearn, who had been lying absolutely motionless with her eyelids tightly shut, opened her eyes and called out in a voice that sounded like an army sergeant's, "Josh, stop that racket, stop it right this minute, y'hear!" Instantly the growling stopped.

Mrs. O'Hearn turned her head to the right. Glaring up at Father Hussey she said, "And what the devil do you think *you're* doing, may I ask?"

Father Hussey seemed completely taken aback. "Why ... why," he stammered, "I was called by your dear niece to ... to — "

"To what?" the old woman demanded. "To give me my

last rites? Are you people out of your minds?" Josh, the dog under the bed, let out a much louder growl this time, one that sounded threatening, followed by a sharp bark. "Josh!" Mrs. O'Hearn shouted, "if you don't behave yourself I'm sending you to the pound this very day. Now shut up!"

Poor Father Hussey, who had bent over Mrs. O'Hearn intending to do something with the little bottle of liquid (I later learned it was called anointing her with holy water) straightened himself and took a step back. I don't know what surprised me more, the strength in the old lady's voice or the suddenness with which Josh obeyed her.

"That's more like it," Mrs. O'Hearn said, satisfied that she'd managed to restore order. "Now, then — " She turned to the priest. "Do me a favour, Father — "

"Of course, dear lady," said the priest.

"Take your solemn look, your bottle of whatever's in there and all the rest of your paraphernalia, and be so kind as to clear out of here until *I* call you. Is that understood?"

From under the bed another growl could be heard, very soft this time, as though Josh approved his mistress' latest command.

Without another word, Father Hussey gathered up his religious accessories and started out of the bedroom, giving my grandfather a sly wink as he departed.

Now the old lady turned her attention to the trio standing to her left. "You three, I've got private business here with Ira Lamport so you needn't stay. I'm sure you can find something to do with yourselves that's more productive than standing guard at my bedside."

Another growl of approval came from somewhere under the bed.

Priscilla, the niece, started to say, "But Auntie — "

"Don't 'but Auntie' me, Priscilla," Mrs. O'Hearn snapped. "And don't look so worried. You and your two brothers here will still do quite nicely after I'm boxed and laid away."

For the first time since we'd entered her bedroom, the old lady acknowledged our presence. "Ira, I think you know my niece Priscilla Cranbrooke and my nephews Dennis and Harold Medley — "

"Yes, indeed, Rebecca, you've spoken of them often."

There was something in the way Gramps said this, and the way Mrs. O'Hearn's thin colourless lips twitched at the corners, like some secret signal, that told me the two of them — Grandfather and his elderly client — had engaged in many soul-searching deliberations in recent times concerning the future welfare of these three relatives.

Mrs. O'Hearn returned to her niece. "Very well, Priscilla, you and your brothers can say goodbye now. Out of here, the three of you."

"We'll drop in on you later, Aunt Rebecca," Harold Medley said.

"That won't be necessary," Mrs. O'Hearn told him firmly. "Besides, you and your brother would probably find it more profitable to drop into an employment agency and get yourselves some jobs. Take your sister along, too. High time *she* found a worthwhile occupation now that her husband's left her."

Looking sheepish, Priscilla, Dennis and Harold filed out, leaving my grandfather and me standing a bit awkwardly at the foot of the bed, and Josh still out of sight somewhere under the bed.

"Who's the child?" Mrs. O'Hearn asked, fixing me with a steely squint.

"My grandson, Rebecca. Ben Marshall. Ben's from Toronto."

"He the one staying with you for the summer?"

"Yes, Rebecca. I thought it'd be nice if he met you and had a look around the estate. Kids from big cities don't get too many opportunities to visit a fine country spread like O'Hearn Estate."

The old woman took a moment to look me over, as though wondering whether or not to hire me as a farmhand or stable boy.

"Very well, Ben. I've some important business to discuss with your grandfather. Do me a favour, please. Get Josh out from under the bed, take him down with you to the kitchen, tell Mrs. Tidy to give the two of you some refreshments."

It hadn't taken me long to conclude that whenever Mrs. O'Hearn issued an order, nobody argued with her. You did what you were commanded to do, and that was that. Still, given all the hostile sounds that had come from that invisible space under her bed, I wasn't eager to get down on my knees and attempt to entice Josh, whom I'd never even laid eyes on, to abandon his hideaway. I had visions of an animal with a nasty temper, snapping jaws, bared teeth, his rear haunches raised as if to spring at me the moment he was out in the open. I searched Gramps' face hoping that perhaps he'd come to my rescue and take the responsibility of luring Josh out of his place of concealment. But Grandfather's face was expressionless, making it clear that I was on my own.

Cautiously, I bent so that I was squatting, but I was not down on my knees, not yet. In a half-hearted voice, I called out, "Here, Josh, c'mon boy." This was met with another one of those unfriendly rumbling noises.

I'd heard my parents refer to certain people as being anti-social, but Josh was now beginning to convince me that dogs — at least *some* dogs — shared that human characteristic. I had never had a dog of my own (my parents explained that our household was too busy to accommodate a full-time burden such as a pet) but I had always yearned for one, preferably a big outdoor kind of dog, maybe a golden retriever or one of those floppy sheepdogs that look windblown even on days when there isn't so much as a stray breeze stirring the air. Although I'd been taught to show a healthy respect for strange dogs, I'd never been particularly afraid of dogs.

Still squatting, still being very careful, I called out once more, "Josh, c'mere boy. There's a good dog."

Another growl, followed by a sharp yap. The last-mentioned sound seemed to be telling me in no uncertain terms to mind my own business and back off.

I stood up. "I'm sorry," I said quietly to Mrs. O'Hearn. "I don't think he likes me."

"Of course he doesn't like you," the old lady said in her matter-of-fact way. "He's no fool, you know. You have to make him a deal, otherwise you can call after him from now till doomsday and he won't budge."

"A deal?" I asked. I wondered what sort of a deal one offered a dog. Whenever adults spoke of "deals" they usually meant money. Could this stubborn dog under the old lady's bed actually be holding out, expecting some kind of bribe? "I don't understand," I said. My tone of voice was really meek by now, partly because Mrs. O'Hearn's voice — despite her weakness and age — was so intimidating, and partly because her dog's voice was anything but heart-warming. "What am I supposed to say to Josh?"

Unexpectedly, Mrs. O'Hearn lowered her voice almost to a whisper. "You say the magic words, that's what."

"Magic words?"

"Yes," she said, then with a brusque motion of her right hand, she beckoned me to come close. Still speaking in a low voice, Mrs. O'Hearn said, "Mrs. Tidy's shortbread cookies … offer him one. Just call out 'shortbread cookie,' then see what happens. But you have to get right down to his level, boy. That half-crouch of yours will never do."

Reluctantly, I got down on my knees, as though I was about to pray. Warily, I peered under the bed, into the darkness there, and said, speaking gently, "Josh … shortbread cookie?"

"No, no, no," Mrs. O'Hearn said testily. "Don't ask him, *tell* him. He's a dog, boy. He's got to be *told*."

I peered once again into the gloom beneath Mrs. O'Hearn's massive bed. In a firmer voice I called out, "Okay, Josh, it's shortbread cookie time. Come!"

I didn't dare take my eyes off the cramped quarters where Josh had seen fit to conceal himself. I figured any second now he might come springing out, and I prepared to defend myself, my arms poised in front of me for protection.

The old lady was right. The magic words worked. Suddenly I caught sight of Josh for the first time. He was edging forward on his belly, being every bit as cautious as I was. It didn't take more than a moment or two before he was totally visible, ready to emerge into the light of day.

Once he was free of the hiding place and completely exposed, the dog stretched himself, splaying his front legs and hind legs the way dogs do, then rising to his full height, his head erect, tail neither up nor down but at half-mast, as though he were still deciding whether or not to be sociable.

It turned out that the dog now staring me in the face (remember, I was still down on my knees with my own face close to the carpeted floor), the fearsome beast now standing before me, was no more than eight inches in height and maybe a foot or so in length. His head seemed to consist of two over-sized brown eyes and nothing else. If it hadn't been for the presence of a sparse crop of greyish whiskers, I would have figured Josh was the only dog in the world without a mouth. His tail was much too long for his body. As for the body, it was a plain, rather dull brown colour without a single inter-esting marking anywhere, not even a tiny white spot. If his tail was too long, it could also be said that his legs were too short, the kind of legs that wouldn't even carry him trouble-free through a shallow puddle after a rainstorm.

I tried to remember where I'd seen dogs like Josh before. Yes, I did remember … in cartoons sometimes. In a movie on television once. A couple of times, too, in the form of dainty porcelain figurines that sat on people's coffee tables or on the mantels of their fireplaces. He was the kind of dog people considered to be a household ornament, the kind of dog that sat on your lap if he liked you, yapped his head off if he didn't, and generally lived from meal to meal without much real use around the place. He was the kind of dog that, even if he'd been the last one in the humane society's shelter, I wouldn't have picked. Wouldn't have taken him home, even for free!

Mrs. O'Hearn's dog, Josh, was — of all things — a Chihuahua.

# Four

So there we were, Mrs. Tidy and I, sitting at the kitchen work table, its bare butcher-block top — like everything else in that room — scrubbed to within an inch of its life. The only thing on the tabletop was a plate of shortbread cookies so fresh out of the oven they were still warm. I could smell their buttery goodness. "Go ahead, son," Mrs. Tidy said, pushing the plate toward me, "have another. They won't ruin your dinner, I promise." I took another, then watched as Mrs. O'Hearn's housekeeper broke one of the cookies into three small pieces and offered them to Josh.

Josh, too, was seated at the table, on a chair between mine and Mrs. Tidy's. Except for the occasional barely audible squeal — which I took to be a squeal of satisfaction — followed by prolonged licking of his chops, Josh sat quietly and calmly. What this proved, I supposed, was that, while some dogs were most contented when chasing squirrels in parks, or racing down country lanes as fast as their four legs could carry them or rounding up stray sheep on the broad fields of cattle farms, a dog like Josh found happiness perched on a kitchen chair doing nothing more exciting or energetic than sniffing for leftover cookie crumbs. Well, maybe old ladies relished that kind of canine companion, but I couldn't picture myself doing any of the things with a pipsqueak like Josh that I dreamed of doing some day when I was independent enough to choose a dog of my own.

To be honest , I think Josh had similar feelings at the time about me. He must have sensed my indifference toward him, for he showed little or no interest whatever in me, a case of tit for tat.

Two or three times I ventured to break the ice between us by extending my hand to pat his head, which wasn't much bigger than a tennis ball. But each time I made a motion in his direction Josh drew back, eyed me suspiciously and split the kitchen air with a bark that would have made a polar bear sit up and take respectful notice. If there was a playful side to this Chihuahua, he must have buried it somewhere well beyond reach in that gloomy recess under his mistress' fortress-like bed.

The only thing we shared, Josh and I, was an insatiable appetite for Mrs. Tidy's extraordinary shortbread cookies. After consuming two and washing them down with homemade lemonade, I went through the motions of politely refusing a third, then a fourth, pretending after each refusal to give in. Josh, on the other hand, was thoroughly ill-mannered. With a sudden burst of energy he leapt from his chair onto the table and snatched his second cookie from the unguarded plate, all the while giving the housekeeper a defiant look, as though daring her to object.

"Does he do that sort of thing often?" I asked Mrs. Tidy.

"Oh, don't mind him," she replied good-naturedly. "Face it; when you get to be Josh's age, you have certain prerogatives."

"Pre-*what*?"

"Prerogatives. Rights, privileges. Antics that others simply have to put up with."

"How old is he?"

Mrs. Tidy paused to recall, casting her gaze up at the ceiling of the kitchen. "Let me see, Mrs. O'Hearn got him at the pound in Port Sanford the very day of the big storm, in fact it was a tornado. That was back in '51, July it was. Talk about wind and rain and hailstones! There was damage all over the place but the worst was when a concrete retaining wall outside the entrance to the large barn collapsed. Mrs. O'Hearn — she's a Bible person, you know, Old Testament, New Testament, she can recite chapter and verse — anyway, like the song says, the wall came tumbling down the day she picked out this little creature here at the pound. So, she decided to call him Joshua. Trouble is, most folks around here don't like names with three syllables so 'Joshua' became 'Josh.' He was a puppy then, no more'n a coupla weeks old. Yessir, that was ten years ago. In Dogland, that's the equivalent of seventy-seven human years, or so they say."

I'm afraid my attitude toward Josh wasn't as tolerant and charitable as Mrs. Tidy's. "My grandfather," I said, "is almost as old as Josh. You wouldn't catch *him* acting up the way this dog acts up, not in a million years, I bet."

Mrs. Tidy's face took on a serious look. "Well now, young man, I'm not sure that's a fair thing to do, comparing this little old Chihuahua here to a human being. You have to remember something, Ben: dogs reach a certain level, yes, but in a sense they never really grow up. You can't apply the same standards of behaviour to Josh that you would to Ira Lamport. Besides, that grandpa of yours is a very special person, not just here at O'Hearn Estate but all over this part of the country. But I'm sure you must know that fact already."

"Not really," I said. "What I mean is, I know he's been a lawyer most of his life, and my mom's told me that he's pretty important to a lot of people around Port Sanford. But we've never had much conversation between the two of us about what exactly he does for people. My dad doesn't much care for Gramps. I don't think the two of them ever got along. Mom says that's because they have similar personalities. Anyway, before I came up here to spend the summer with Gramps, Dad warned me not to expect a lot of heart-to-heart talks. He called Gramps a cold fish."

Mrs. Tidy looked shocked. "Ira Lamport a cold fish? Good heavens, that couldn't be further from the truth, Ben. It's just that, well, he makes great demands on himself. You might say he's a perfectionist. Yes, that's his reputation, Ben. The man's a perfectionist." Mrs. Tidy laughed to herself. "God knows, he'd have to be a perfectionist to earn Mrs. O'Hearn's affection and respect. He's done legal work for me and my husband, too. Talk about dotting your I's and crossing your T's! Ira Lamport wouldn't know how to cut a corner if his life depended on it."

I have to admit that Mrs. Tidy's opinion of Gramps aroused a certain feeling of pride in me, but that feeling fell far short of love. Maybe it was because so much of the time, even at the dinner table, there was that arrogant tilt of his head, that piercing gaze of his eyes, the no-nonsense way he had of putting things, that made easygoing small talk between the two of us virtually impossible.

There must have been something about my reaction to what Mrs. Tidy was telling me — perhaps I shrugged, or shook my head or simply looked unimpressed — that made her put down her glass of lemonade and lean closer to me. "I'm going to let you in on a little secret about your Grandpa, Ben, but don't you ever let on to him that I told you. Promise?"

"Promise."

"Very well, then. Bill — that's my husband, of course — Bill and me got ourselves into a pack of trouble one time about a dozen or so years ago. That was before we got hired to look after Mrs. O'Hearn's property. Bill'd been a bricklayer and hurt his back real bad on the job, and had to quit construction work. I'd been a cook in a little diner just down a piece where Highway 48 runs into 35. Well, Bill being unable to work at his trade, and me having experience in a diner, we figured it'd be a smart thing if we opened a restaurant, the two of us. Anyway, the woman that owned the diner, she heard about our plans and said why didn't we buy her diner, she wanted to retire. So Bill and me, we did just that. We bought the place, lock, stock and barrel as they say. Put every cent we had into it, and then some ... by which I mean we had to borrow from the bank. And we had a grand opening ... big sign out front: 'Welcome To Hilda's Diner.' Free coffee and donuts the first day, lots of people, well-wishers, including your grandfather. Everything looked rosy. Then, what do you think the government ups and does? They decide to change the easterly end of Highway 48 so that it hits 35 at a spot three miles south of our diner. Three whole miles to the south!"

Mrs. Tidy interrupted her narrative for a moment, and glanced in the direction of the circular stairway to make certain my grandfather wasn't on his way down. "I'll make a long story short," she went on. "Before long, business dried up, Bill and me were dead broke, and we had the bank and our suppliers banging at our doors day and night demanding to get paid what we owed them. At one point the bunch of 'em sent out a sheriff's officer — that's like a court official — to seize all our possessions. Guess who stood at the door and prevented that from happening? Ira Lamport, that's who."

"You mean," I said, frowning because something about this tale didn't make sense, "my grandfather stopped this court official from carrying out the law? From what my mother's told me about him, that's not the kind of thing he would do. Mom says a lot of the time my grandfather drives people crazy because he does everything strictly by the book. 'Stickler,' that's the word Mom uses to describe him."

"Oh, but that's exactly the point of my story, don't you see? It's because Ira Lamport's a stickler that he made that sheriff fella back right off." Mrs. Tidy sat back and began to laugh. Her eyes, when she laughed, were transformed from ovals to crinkled crescents, and her chins, for there were two of them, shook as though made of jelly.

"I can see it so clear, Ben," she said, leaning closer again. "Hollis Burden — that was the officer's name — was a scrawny little guy with a face like one of those ferrets you see out in bush country sometimes. You give a little man like that a little power, a little authority, and there's no end to how important he'll try to act. Anyway, Hollis shows up late one afternoon at our doorstep ... I mean, at the door of our diner ... and he pulls out this fancy piece of paper, this court document with a big red seal the size of an apple. But your grandfather — "

Again Mrs. Tidy interrupted her story and half-stood, directing her attention to the section of the foyer near the stairway. "Just want to make sure," she said, "your grandfather isn't on his way down. He mightn't be too pleased, me telling all this stuff about him and Hollis Burden. He's not one to be boasting about himself, and I've seen him get downright embarrassed, even displeased, whenever people praise him openly, in public especially."

Satisfied that Gramps was still occupied upstairs with Mrs. O'Hearn, Mrs. Tidy carried on. "Now where was I? Oh, yes, like I said, there's Hollis Burden playing wolf, and he's got this impressive-looking document that he's starting to read, sounding like those town criers you see in the movies ... 'Hear ye, hear ye' and 'Whereas' and stuffy-sounding legal words like that ... but before Hollis can get ten words out of his mealy little mouth, your grandfather shouts — God, Ben, it was like a clap of thunder bounding off a mountaintop! — Ira booms out: 'Now just a damn minute, Hollis Burden, I'm the lawyer for these folks, the Tidys, and I've got a right to check that document you're holding in your hands before you take one more step into this place. I'll give you exactly two seconds to hand me that piece of paper, do you understand?'

"Well, Hollis Burden understood all right. You could see him buckling at the knees and his hands were shaking as he handed the court order up to Ira. And Ira stood there in the doorway, blocking Burden from entering, Ira looking like a sentry, only things missing were a rifle and a battle helmet. And Ira gets this look on his face, like a terrible black cloud passing over the land the second before a storm breaks out. Again he says, in that booming voice of his, to Hollis, 'Who the devil are William and Hilda Tiny?' And Hollis says, 'That's *Tidy*, not Tiny.' And your grandfather practically slams that document in Hollis Burden's face, he points to the names near the top, and repeats his question, 'Who are Mr. and Mrs. *Tiny*, I'd like to know?'

"So Hollis puts on his glasses, and stares at the court paper and sure enough they got our names down as 'Tiny' instead of 'Tidy.' And Hollis gets cute right away and says 'C'mon, Mr. Lamport, this really refers to your clients, Bill and Hilda Tidy, everybody with half a brain'd know that.' And your grandfather says to Hollis, 'Well, you just trek right back to wherever you got this sloppy piece of work and put the other half of your brain to good use. Meantime, this order is not enforceable and you're not to touch one stick of furniture nor one piece of equipment in this restaurant!'

"Well, Ben, I don't have to tell you, Hollis Burden was a mighty unhappy man. Seems at that hour, late on a Friday, there was no way he could go back to the courthouse, find the judge and correct the mistake in that document. So Hollis decides to brazen it out. 'I'm heading back to Port Sanford to fetch the chief of police,' he says to your grandfather. 'This here's a court order, and you're obstructing justice, Ira Lamport. You can be arrested because that's a criminal offence.' And your grandfather just stood there not budging an inch, filling that doorway like a brick wall. 'You can bring the Queen of England for all I care,' Ira says, 'but you're not going to set so much as the toe of your boot in this place.'

"And you know what, Ben? Hollis tucked his tail between his legs and drove off, muttering words I wouldn't repeat to a young fella like yourself. And we figured he might sneak back later, hoping we'd gone home, and break into the diner, grab our property. But I guess he lost his nerve. Next day, Saturday morning, a group of our creditors ... people we owed money to, including our bank manager ... came out to the diner. And your grandfather was there because he'd stayed the night with us ... yes, Ben, the entire night! And by golly, we made a deal to head off the sheriff, and pay our creditors so much on the dollar over a period of time. Ira Lamport saved our skins that weekend. More'n that, he saved our lives, because we thought we'd come to the end of everything. So, is your grandfather a stickler? You bet he is, Ben."

Just then we heard my grandfather coming down the circular stairway. His footsteps sounded slow and heavy. Quickly the housekeeper pulled her apron away from her eyes, dabbed away the moisture from her ruddy cheeks and straightened herself in her chair, forcing a brave smile as Gramps entered the kitchen.

"Can I offer you some refreshment, Mr. Lamport?" she said, her voice cheerful again.

For a moment Grandfather stood in the middle of the

kitchen, as though he hadn't heard a word the housekeeper had said to him. He seemed distracted and his shoulders sagged a bit. He set down his weather-beaten leather briefcase, and it too seemed to sag there at his feet, like a tired-out old mongrel.

"Some shortbread and a cool glass of lemonade?" Mrs. Tidy urged.

At last Gramps snapped out of what looked like a trance. Ignoring the housekeeper's friendly offer, which struck me at the time as rude on his part, he looked over at me. "We better get going, Ben. I've got a lot to do back at the office, and not much time to do it in."

There seemed to be no limit to Mrs. Tidy's good nature. "Let me fix a small package of cookies for you and your grandson, Mr. Lamport. It'll only take a minute."

But Grandfather was in no mood for shortbread or lemonade or anything of the sort at that moment. In a tone of voice I'd never heard him use before, speaking as though much of his spirit had been drained from him, he said, "There are times when I wish I'd never heard of the law and just stayed a farmer like my father and his father before him."

Mrs. Tidy knew better than to bring up the matter of cookies again. As for me, I did the wise thing and kept my mouth shut as I followed Grandfather out to the car. In fact, we didn't say a word to one another all the way back to Port Sanford. I kept thinking that it was a lucky thing there were no police cruisers in sight, for Grandfather broke the speed limit from one end of the route to the other on that return journey.

# Five

It was a little after four o'clock when we arrived back at my grandfather's house in Port Sanford. His secretary, Miss Trimble, met us on the front porch. "I was just about to leave for the day," she said to Grandfather. "I've left today's dictation on your desk, Mr. Lamport, for you to look over." She held a small bundle of envelopes in one hand, her purse in the other. "I'll drop the mail off at the post office on my way."

"I need a favour, Agnes," Grandfather said to his secretary. "I know it's your normal quitting time, but Mrs. O'Hearn's done it again."

Miss Trimble let out a long sigh and she bit her lower lip. But there was also a look of amusement in her eyes. "How many times has she done this? I've lost count."

My grandfather looked grim now. "This time it's for real, Agnes. She really is going. I've spoken with Doc Kirkland. Her temperature's all over the thermometer and her heartbeat's getting more and more irregular."

Miss Trimble needed no further explanation. "I'll call my mother, tell her I'm going to be late for supper." She followed Gramps back into the house and into his office.

"Ben," Grandfather called to me, "please tell Mrs. Bjorklund not to hold dinner for me. We're going to be tied up here for

a while, I'm not certain how long, then I have to scoot back
out to Mrs. O'Hearn's."

"Tonight?"

"Yes, Ben, tonight. Now you'll have to excuse us."

Without another word my grandfather brought the sliding oak doors together.

Ever since the first day I'd arrived here, there was something about the way those doors came together tightly that
made me feel shut out, that told me that I was a visitor, but
that I was not really a part of my grandfather's life. I was comfortable here, safe, well-fed, all my needs were attended to here,
even my laundry. But Mrs. Bjorklund, unlike Mrs. O'Hearn's
housekeeper, was a woman of few words. Every day she went
about her work efficiently cleaning the house, preparing
meals, leaving everything immaculate after dinner before
returning to her own home for the night. Businesslike, that's
what she was. In fact, my father's description of my grandfather — "a cold fish" — best described Mrs. Bjorklund's
personality. It amazed me that a woman with such a cut-and-
dried attitude about things could turn out such appetizing meals
three times a day. Even her breakfasts resembled photographs
in food magazines.

With my grandfather and his secretary preoccupied in the
office, and Mrs. Bjorklund going about her tasks — which at
the moment consisted of polishing the mahogany sideboard
and china cabinet in the dining room for what must have been
the millionth time — I sensed that I was bound for yet another
boring evening in the town of Port Sanford. There seemed little reason to bike downtown. At this hour most of the shops
were getting ready to close for the night and the streets would
be deserted. There was a variety store on the main street with
a pinball machine, but I learned early on that the place was a
kind of sacred territory, by which I mean that a gang of

teenagers from the local high school staked their claim to the pinball machine every afternoon, even during summer holidays, and outsiders like me were definitely not welcome.

It was at times like this that I would have given anything for the company of a dog. Not a dog like Josh, I need hardly point out. I mean a *real* dog, the kind I described before. Maybe Mrs. Tidy was correct about dogs, that they grow *old* but not *up*; then again, maybe she was wrong. After all, thousands and thousands of people had dogs. Why not me?

I ate dinner alone that evening at the big mahogany table in the dining room. (Mrs. Bjorklund delivered a platter of sandwiches and a pot of coffee to Gramps and Miss Trimble, still working away behind those closed doors.) From time to time the doors would open just a crack and I could hear my grandfather dictating, and his secretary tapping away at her old-fashioned typewriter with such speed that the sound reminded me of a machine gun. The only other sound in the house was the steady ticking of the grandfather clock in the hallway just off the dining room. Every half-hour the clock's chimes rang out so loudly I imagined people miles away could hear them and thought they were church bells calling them to prayer. The only joke I'd heard my grandfather make since I'd arrived in Port Sanford was about that clock. Pointing to it, he said, "Well, now we've got Big Ben — " Then, jerking his thumb in my direction, he added, "And Little Ben." His housekeeper, standing nearby, smiled at this. Her smile was like an iceberg cracking in two.

I had just finished a slice of Mrs. Bjorklund's lemon-and-poppyseed cake when the doors to Grandfather's office opened wide and both he and his secretary emerged. He was carrying a file with a sheaf of papers between its covers, and Miss Trimble was following close behind holding open that faithful old briefcase. "Here," she said, "let me stuff that file into your briefcase, Mr. Lamport. We don't want you losing any of these papers, do we?"

Watching her tuck the file into his briefcase, my grandfather looked impatient. There was a sense of urgency about the way he snapped the locks shut on the briefcase. Mrs. Bjorklund had come out to the front hall. "More sandwiches or coffee?" she asked.

"No time," Gramps said. "Gotta head right back to O'Hearn's."

"What about your hat?" Mrs. Bjorklund said.

"Why would I need a hat?" Grandfather snapped. "Sun's been down for an hour."

"You'd best take an umbrella, then," the housekeeper said, sounding as though she was my grandfather's mother. "They're calling for rain, heavy at times, later on tonight."

"Since when was I ever bothered by rain?" Gramps demanded. For the first time, I was beginning to feel a little sympathy for his housekeeper. No matter what she suggested, his responses sounded as though he was ready to bite off her head.

Given the foul mood he was in, it took more nerve than I thought I possessed for me to ask, "Can I go along with you, Gramps?" It wasn't that I was eager to return to the O'Hearn estate. It's just that a trip back there was better than hanging about Grandfather's house all evening with nobody to talk to. True, there was a television set in the den on the second floor but the programs this time of year were mostly reruns.

Gruffly, Gramps replied, "Come along if you've nothing better to do. But be quick about it, Ben. I've not a minute to waste."

As before, we covered the distance between Port Sanford and the O'Hearn estate without conversation, the silence broken only by my grandfather's contempt for the skills of other motorists on the highway. He grumbled when they travelled too fast, when they travelled too slowly, when they made turns or switched lanes, when they stopped and when they started up again. Nothing they did satisfied him. I thought of what Mrs. Tidy had said about him, that he was a perfectionist. And I thought to myself, if this is what happens to perfectionists, then some day I'm going to be as *im*perfect as I can be.

We pulled into the O'Hearn driveway. To my surprise there were more cars parked in front of the big house than earlier in the day when we'd paid our initial visit.

One of them, a black two-door coupe, looked familiar. "It looks like that priest has come back," I said.

"That green four-wheel drive over there belongs to Doc Kirkland," my grandfather said. "I don't like the look of this," he said, getting out of the car.

The front door of the O'Hearn house had been left open and Mrs. Tidy stood there, the bright lights of the foyer outlining her plump silhouette. It was only when we drew close and could see the features of her face that we noticed tears in her eyes and running down her cheeks. "I'm afraid you're too late, Mr. Lamport," she said. "She's passed on. Just like that. Here one minute, gone the next, poor soul."

# Six

**M**rs. Bjorklund's weather forecast turned out to be correct. In fact, her prediction of heavy rain was an understatement. Sheets of rain flung themselves against the hood and windshield of Grandfather's old Buick as we made our way back to Port Sanford. Flashes of lightning lit up the road before us brilliantly, turning the black pavement each time into a blinding strip of silver for a split second, exposing the farmers' fields on either side in an eerie bluish glow. Loud claps of thunder interrupted the steady monotonous rhythm of the windshield wipers, the two noises, one irregular, the other regular, together forming a kind of dirge. The sights and sounds of that return trip to town matched my grandfather's mood so perfectly one would have thought he'd ordered them.

The angry look on his face that greeted the news of Mrs. O'Hearn's death, back at her estate, remained on Gramps' face all the way back to Port Sanford. Again I had the feeling that he was blaming himself for something, something terribly important either to Mrs. O'Hearn, or to himself, or maybe to both of them. Every once in a while he would slap the steering wheel, a gesture I took to be one of disgust or deep disappointment.

It wasn't until we'd pulled into the driveway of Gramps'

house that I had the courage to speak up. "Gramps?" I began gingerly, just with that one word — Gramps — like a person sticking a toe into a river of freezing water, testing. At first there was no response. My grandfather sat behind the wheel, with the engine turned off, staring straight ahead, with a stony expression. "Gramps?" I said again, quietly.

At last he spoke up. "What is it?"

"Did something go wrong … I mean back there at the O'Hearn place? You look like — " I hesitated.

"Like what?"

At this point, I plugged my nose and dove right into the icy current. "You look like you just lost your best friend in the whole world."

There was a long pause. Grandfather maintained that stare and I began to wonder if we were going to spend the rest of the night right there in the driveway, with him brooding in silence and me watching him out of the corner of my eye. He turned to me and fixed those piercing eyes of his on me for a full minute, without uttering a sound. Then he looked away again, and went back to staring down the driveway, as though somewhere down at the far end there was a bundle of memories that was suddenly opening up to him. He began to speak, his words coming slowly, not the strong authoritative decisive voice of the lawyer giving dictation to his secretary, but the low halting voice of a man who — as Mrs. Tidy had put it back there at the O'Hearn place — might be here one minute, gone the next.

"Maybe you're old enough to understand some fundamental things about life. You *are* going on thirteen, aren't you?" I'd passed my thirteenth birthday months earlier, but this wasn't the time to quibble.

"Anyway, as I started to say, when I was thirteen, going on fourteen, being the only boy in our family — I had two younger sisters, your Great-aunts Ruby and Merle — being the only boy I was put in charge of the team of horses my father used for plowing.

"Winter came on, the first winter I would be looking after Eb and Zeb. Winters in those days seemed much colder than they do nowadays, and my dad constructed a stove in the horse barn to keep Eb and Zeb as warm as possible. One of my chores was to load up the stove at night before we went to bed, make sure there was plenty of wood so it would burn most of the night, make sure the damper in the main chimney pipe was open so the fire would feed properly and the smoke rise up.

"Well, one night in February — bitterly cold, so cold that when you talked out in the open your words seemed to turn into icicles in front of your face — that night I guess I was in a hurry to stoke the stove in the barn and get into the house as fast as I could and jump into a nice warm bed. In my rush, maybe I overlooked to make sure the damper was fully open. To this day, I'm not certain what I did, or didn't do — "

I knew it would end with disaster and I really didn't want to hear about it. But Gramps was determined to finish his story. "We'd barely fallen asleep, the whole family, when a noise floated across the yard, an awful noise coming from the horse barn. It was Eb and Zeb, screaming in that high-pitched way that horses scream when they're terrified. There was a bright orange and red glow lighting up the barnyard. The horse barn was ablaze, going up like a Roman candle. We rushed out in our nightclothes — I didn't bother to put on my boots, just rushed out in the snow in my bare feet — but it was no use. In minutes they were goners, Eb and Zeb. My dad looked right then as if his own world had just gone up in smoke and flames. But the worst part for me was what he said. He didn't shout, didn't rant or rave, or stamp his feet and throw his arms about the way some men might've in that situation. All he said, so quiet I could scarcely hear his words … all he said to me was, 'You didn't double-check the damper, did you?'

"My mother, she was standing close by, she came over and put an arm around my shoulder and we watched the horse barn disappear into the night air in a cloud of sparks and cinders. And she said, 'It's all right, Ira, nobody's perfect, not even God, or He wouldn't have let this happen.'

"She meant well, my mother did, but that wasn't good enough for me. And the events of that night, for better or worse, stayed with me for the rest of my youth, and schooling, and years of practising law."

I waited a moment, then asked, "Is that why they say you're a perfectionist?"

Gramps looked straight at me. "*Who* says?"

Too late to retreat, I thought. I'd already put one foot in my mouth, I might as well put the other. "People say."

"What people?"

"Mom. Mrs. Tidy. And I can tell Miss Trimble and Mrs. Bjorklund think you're a perfectionist just by the way they try to do things to please you."

If there was such a thing as a person with three feet, then I guess I would have put all three into my mouth, for I added, without really giving much thought to what I was saying, "And maybe that's why my dad thinks you're a cold fish, too."

Then, to my complete astonishment, Grandfather threw back his head and let out a single loud laugh. "Well, that certainly proves the old saying: It takes one to know one. I've always thought your father had the insides of a refrigerator. And *he* thinks *I'm* cold! Well, I'll be damned!"

"But it's true, isn't it, Gramps?"

"What's true?"

"That you're a stickler, like Mom says."

"Maybe. What of it?"

"Is that why you seem so disgusted? Are you blaming yourself because Mrs. O'Hearn died? Was it your fault she died?"

"Of course not."

"Then I don't get it. You looked back there, and even all the way here, like you were blaming yourself for something bad that happened, like you were guilty."

Grandfather's voice turned frosty. "You wouldn't understand," he said. He looked away, as though distancing himself from me.

"That doesn't make sense," I said. "Five minutes ago you said I was old enough now to begin to understand some pretty fundamental things about life."

"Don't you go putting words in my mouth, young man," Gramps said gruffly.

"I'm not putting words in your mouth," I protested. "Those were your very words. Now, suddenly, you've changed your mind."

Gramps shot me a look that showed he was very annoyed. "I can't believe I'm sitting here arguing with a thirteen-year-old," he said.

"Isn't that what lawyers do, argue?"

"Not with *kids*, for God's sake."

"I'm not just a kid. You said so yourself."

"Well, you're not exactly an adult either, so don't let what I told you go to your head, young man. A thirteen-year-old's got to know his place."

Now *I* was the one who was angry. "My place? My *place*? My 'place' is at your place. And I'm your flesh and blood, at least that's what Mom said to me when I told her I wasn't sure about spending the summer here in Port Sanford. I'm no happier being here than you are having me here. But the least we can do is *talk* to each other."

"That's no way to talk to a person who's giving you a roof over your head and three meals a day — "

"You really *are* what my dad said you are ... a cold fish!"

"That's a lie!" Gramps yelled, "A damn lie!"

"Then prove you're not. Why're you so upset about Mrs. O'Hearn's death?"

Without a moment's hesitation, my grandfather blurted out, "Because now I've got to kill her dog!"

There was a long pause. Seated inside the car, we could hear only the last raindrops falling on the windshield, signalling the end of the storm. Beads of rain were still collected on the hood of the Buick, and in the darkness they looked like tiny fading pearls, or diamonds that were losing their twinkle.

I couldn't believe what I'd just heard, and my first instinct was to utter an incredulous laugh. "You've got to do *what*?" I said.

"Kill her dog. Kill Josh," Grandfather said.

I laughed again.

"It's not funny," my grandfather said, fixing me with a cold look. "It's not funny at all. And that's only part of the mess. But it's the worst part in some ways. And worst of all, I've just committed one of the greatest sins a lawyer can commit. I've just violated the rule of confidentiality."

"The rule of confidentiality?"

"Yes, the most sacred rule, the most sacred trust between a lawyer and his client. And it's your fault, Ben. You goaded me into it. Now let's get out of this car and into the house before you lead me further into temptation."

I did as Grandfather commanded. I got out of the car and marched into the house after him. But now my own anger was something that couldn't be shed, like clothing at bedtime. I was determined to get to the bottom of this business between my grandfather and Mrs. O'Hearn, even if it meant that next morning Gramps would send me packing.

# Seven

Grandfather no doubt figured once inside his house he could very conveniently escape into his private cave — which is what his office amounted to in my view — and avoid further interrogation from his pesky grandson. But I wasn't about to let him get away with a stunt like that. Before he had a chance to slam those heavy oak sliding doors together, I'd managed to slip behind him and station myself in the narrow space between the doors so that he couldn't make a sudden exit. He was trapped. He did not resign himself to his arrest gracefully. He stood in the centre of the threadbare Persian rug, directly beneath a chandelier that must have been assembled when the light bulb was first invented. (Come to think of it, everything in Grandfather's office looked as though it was in fashion a hundred years earlier.) Hands on his hips, legs apart, he stood there glaring down at me, the dim overhead light giving his expression an extra measure of fierceness.

"Tell me about the dog," I insisted. "Why must you put him down?"

"I'm not the one who's actually got to put the dog down," my grandfather shouted impatiently. "My job is to take him to the veterinarian, Dr. Hetherington. That's the vet's job, don't you understand?"

"No, I don't," I said. "I've never murdered an animal, only flies and mosquitoes."

"Don't get smart with me, young man," Gramps shot back. "If there's one thing I can do without right now it's snide comments from a thirteen-year-old."

"But you're always saying how precious life is. Now you're going to arrange to have that puny little runt — "

"Josh is *not* a puny little runt. He's a fine example of his breed. What's more, that 'runt' gave old Mrs. O'Hearn ten years of loyalty and pleasure."

"Then why must he die?"

"Because her will says so, that's why!" Grandfather blurted out.

"But I heard you and Miss Trimble talking before about how the old lady kept changing her will all the time. How come you didn't talk her out of having her dog done away with?"

Gramps dropped his arms to his sides and shook his head slowly from side to side. I took these movements to be a sign of defeat, or at least a signal that I had him cornered.

Still glaring at me, he said, "You know you're more persistent than a toothache, don't you?"

Secretly I was overjoyed to hear this, even though it was not intended to be a compliment. Better, I thought, to be a toothache than to be ignored. "Yes," I said agreeably, "I know."

"You've got all the worst characteristics of your mother … stubborn, disrespectful of your elders, argumentative. What's more, you've inherited your father's lack of charm."

I nodded my head. "You're right," I said, more agreeably than before.

"Very well, as long as we have your shortcomings clearly stated for the record," Grandfather said, solemnly, like a judge.

"Fine," I said. "If you're happy, I'm happy."

Gramps moved to the back of his desk and sat down in his

swivel chair, groaning as he worked his frame into the seat, the old chair itself creaking just as loudly as it prepared to bear his weight. "Some day," he muttered, "I'm gonna heave this thing into the lake down at the foot of the town dock. Trouble is, it's been with me so long it'd probably float right back." He motioned me to come forward from my sentry post between the sliding doors. "You might as well sit down," he said grudgingly, pointing to an armchair on the opposite side of the desk.

It was the first time since my arrival in Port Sanford that I'd had an opportunity to take a seat in my grandfather's office. "Is this where your clients sit?" I asked.

"You bet it is," Grandfather said, "except they *pay* for the privilege."

"I'd offer to pay you, too," I said, "except all I've got is one month's allowance, and that's probably not enough, from what my dad tells me."

Grandfather's eyes narrowed. "Oh, yeah? And what precisely does your dear papa tell the whole world about *that* particular subject, may I ask?"

I looked my grandfather straight in the eye. "He says he figures you've still got the first dollar you ever made." I detected a slight twitch at the corners of Grandfather's mouth now, as though he was saving up for a private laugh later on when I wasn't around.

Quietly Gramps said, "I think it's well past your bedtime, young man."

I said, brushing off this suggestion, "How come you didn't get Mrs. O'Hearn to change her will ... about the dog, I mean?"

"I can't get into that kind of discussion with you, Ben. Like I said before, lawyers are bound by very strict rules of confidentiality. We don't go telling every Tom, Dick and Harry our clients' business."

"I'm not every Tom, Dick and Harry," I said. "I'm your

grandson. Your only grandchild, for that matter. You said, soon after I came to Port Sanford, that maybe some day I might want to become a lawyer and take over your practice. How can you expect me to know whether or not I'm interested in doing that if you don't fill me in?"

"*Fill you in*! My God, you may be my grandson but you're sure as heck not my *partner*!"

I rose from my chair and looked across the desk at my grandfather. "I think I know why you don't want to talk about it," I said. "I think you screwed up somewhere. Otherwise you wouldn't've stood there in Mrs. Tidy's kitchen saying you wished you'd been a farmer like your dad. And after you found out the old lady had died, you stood there repeating over and over 'damn, damn, damn.' That's it, isn't it? You must've screwed up really bad, right?"

"Wrong!" my grandfather shouted, and brought his fist down hard on his desk, so hard that the crockery mug that held his pens and pencils flipped over on its side, spilling its contents. "What happened is that she made some last-minute changes in her will ... some very, very important changes ... changes that would have done a lot of people in this town a lot of good ... and a change that would have spared Josh's life. But because it took me too long to drive back here to my office and dictate the changes to my secretary, and drive back to the estate to get the new will signed — " Grandfather halted abruptly, then said quietly, "Ach, why am I wasting my time and energy trying to explain this to ... to a *kid*. Go to bed, Ben, please. I need to be alone for a while."

"Just because this Mrs. O'Hearn decided to make a bunch of last-minute changes ... her being so sick and near death and all that ... that's not your fault, then, is it?"

My grandfather leaned forward, resting his elbows on his desk top, his broad bony hands covering his forehead and shading his eyes. Speaking as though only to himself, he said, "Maybe it's my fault. Maybe it's the old woman's fault. Maybe it's God's fault. What matters is that I'm stuck with the will she *did* sign, the one she made a couple of months ago."

"I still don't get it," I said. "You're her lawyer, right? If she told you what she really wanted to do with all her money, isn't that good enough?"

"No, it's not. The law about wills is as old as the mountains. A will has to be signed properly. That means, the person making the will — called the testator — must actually sign, and her signature must be witnessed at the very same time by two witnesses. There are exceptions to this rule. They're called holograph wills, like if a farmer's tractor rolls over and pins him underneath and the farmer manages to scratch his will into the paint on the fender before he dies. Same thing happens to soldiers who are wounded and maybe dying. Really unusual circumstances of that sort. But in Mrs. O'Hearn's case the last will she made just never got signed and that's all there is to it, boy. A ninety-year-old lady lying on her deathbed isn't the same as a farmer whose tractor accidentally tips over on him. So, like I said, her will made a couple of months ago is the only one that counts."

I probably should have taken more time to consider what I had just learned before venturing my next opinion. Unfortunately, I didn't. "If that's the law," I said, "then the law's pretty stupid."

This brought a cold stare that sent a chill right through me even on this warm July night. Grandfather's voice trembled as he said, "Are you presuming to tell me that what I do for a living is *stupid*?"

At that moment, looking at the expression on my grandfather's face, hearing his tone of voice, I would have given anything — including my practically brand-new three-speed bike — for the Persian rug underfoot to swallow me and carry me off like a magic carpet to some faraway deserted island.

"I didn't mean — uh — I mean, what I was trying to say — " I stammered.

My grandfather rose slowly and with some difficulty from his swivel chair. He paused for the longest moment in my memory and seemed to be studying me, as though he'd never before taken the time to see me as I really was. "Let's get one thing straight, son," he said, his voice raspy with fatigue. "You may not think much of me, but so long as you're under my roof and eating three meals a day prepared in my kitchen, I'm entitled to your respect. I make no claim to your love. You don't even have to *like* me. But I won't settle for anything less than your respect. Now I suggest we both turn in before the air around here gets even more electric. Good night."

I'd seen movies and dramas on television where condemned criminals were permitted to say a few words in their own defence before being dispatched to prison but I chose to forgo any such privilege here. I turned and started to make my retreat, getting as far as the sliding doors when Grandfather called after me, "Ben — "

Feeling uneasy, dreading whatever was coming next, I turned to face him. "Yes?"

"You're not entirely wrong, you know. There *are* times when laws are stupid. But we'll have to delve into that subject another day. It's late. Off you go."

There are times when kids, deep inside, have to be satisfied with something less than apologies from their elders.

I went off to bed that night satisfied.

Early the next morning the phone rang twice. The first call was from my mother, the second from my father.

"So, Ben, how's it going between you two?" Mom asked.

"Well, it's like *Perry Mason* on TV. Every time I object, Gramps says I'm over-ruled and that's that."

"You can't say I didn't give you fair warning," my mother

said. "Living with your grandfather was never a bed of roses. Do you think you can stick it out for the next few weeks, Ben?"

"You're leaving for Europe tomorrow. What choice do I have? Yeah, I can stick it out. I've already scored one or two points. Not much, maybe, but I think I can hold my own for a while. I'm obstinate, remember?"

"At the end of the summer you're going to deserve a medal."

"Skip the medal. All I want when I leave here is a break."

There was a long silence at Mom's end of the line. I had the feeling when she said goodbye that she was trying to keep from crying.

A little later my father was on the phone. "I have to make this call short, Ben," he said. "I'm due in the OR in a couple of minutes. A motorcycle accident victim. Two broken legs, a dislocated shoulder, God knows what else. Promise me you'll never ride one of those damn things. How're you doing up there with the old curmudgeon?"

I'd never heard the word "curmudgeon" before, but knowing how my father and grandfather felt about each other, it was easy to figure out that "curmudgeon" was not something you'd call somebody you liked.

"We're getting along," I replied.

"Money holding out?"

"So far so good. If I run short, maybe I can borrow a few dollars from Gramps."

I heard my father snicker. "I wouldn't count on borrowing money from Ira Lamport if I were you. Like they say, he's so tight he squeaks. You let *me* know if you need money. If you can't reach me, just leave a message with my receptionist."

"Thanks, Dad," I said.

"Look after yourself."

"I always do."

# Eight

**M**rs. O'Hearn had died on a Tuesday night and her funeral took place the following Saturday. During the interval between her death and burial, Grandfather's mood became darker by the hour. Nothing appeared to give him any pleasure. The July weather had turned balmy, with sunny afternoons that transformed the well-kept lawns in the neighbourhood into emeralds that shimmered in the heat, the greens accented here and there by beds of flowers bending to and fro under the lazy back-and-forth whoosh of sprinklers. Gentle breezes crossed and re-crossed the broad porch at the side of the house where Gramps sat every evening after dinner in an oversized wicker rocker, smoking his one cigar of the day. I was given to understand that those were very fine cigars, hand-rolled in Cuba and costly. I can still smell the rich pungent aroma they contributed to the night air. My mother had told me cigars were among the few luxuries Grandfather allowed himself (he also enjoyed good Scotch, which he drank modestly before dinner). Still, he took little notice of the sky and the gardens by day, and as darkness settled over him, there in his rocking chair, it seemed as though his thoughts were drifting up and away, like the smoke of his cigar, leaving a kind of emptiness in his life.

Grandfather's housekeeper, Mrs. Bjorklund, went about her business in silence, her daily agenda filled with pots and pans and polishes. As for Miss Trimble, her comings and goings were scarcely noticeable as far as I was concerned. If Mrs. Bjorklund was built like a tree, and Mrs. Tidy like two trees bundled together, Miss Trimble resembled a slim willow branch, one that would easily snap in a stiff wind. My conversations with her were pretty well limited to "Good morning" and "Good evening."

I found myself studying the calendar in my bedroom, running diagonal strokes through the days already past with a thick black marker, and looking forward to that wonderful time when all the days of July and August would be similarly stroked off and I would bid farewell to the town of Port Sanford.

On the Monday morning after Mrs. O'Hearn's funeral, my grandfather said to Mrs. Bjorklund at breakfast, "I'd appreciate if you'd brew up an extra pot of coffee this morning, Mrs. Bjorklund. Oh, yes, and a plate of muffins, too, if you don't mind. I've got some folks due at nine-thirty." Then, in a tone that was unmistakably sarcastic, he said, "I'm sure that your excellent coffee and muffins will serve to relieve their deep grief to some extent." At this, Gramps' housekeeper did something I'd never seen her do since my arrival. She chuckled, but discreetly, of course.

At precisely nine-twenty-nine — as though they had camped overnight on Grandfather's doorstep — in came Priscilla Cranbrooke and her brothers Dennis and Harold Medley. Mrs. Cranbrooke was attired appropriately in a black dress and clutched a black purse. The two men wore black neckties. All three wore sunglasses, and as I caught sight of them entering the front hall and making their way single-file into Grandfather's office, whispering among themselves, they struck me as members of some secret organization who'd come to collect ransom money or steal the formula for some terrible bomb.

The oak doors remained open long enough for me to observe Grandfather rise from behind his desk and greet his visitors. "Good morning," he said. His manner was stiff and formal. There were no handshakes. Only one of the visitors returned Grandfather's greeting. "Good morning to you, sir," Priscilla Cranbrooke said. My grandfather motioned to them to take the three straight-backed chairs he'd arranged for them. "Miss Trimble here has made copies for each of you of your aunt's last will and testament … I mean, the one she signed, of course."

I heard Harold Medley clear his throat, then he said, sounding a bit unsure of himself, "We understand that Aunt Rebecca made a later will … with some — uh — important changes — "

"That's true," Grandfather replied, his voice still cold. "She never got 'round to signing it … unfortunately."

Harold Medley leaned forward and spoke up. "Unfortunately? Why do you say unfortunately?" His tone was sharp now.

My grandfather hesitated before replying. Then I saw him glance toward the oak doors which still stood open. "Miss Trimble," he said to his secretary, "please close the doors."

For the next half-hour or so, I heard their voices rising and falling. Isn't it peculiar how you can remember a conversation almost word for word when the people involved have lost their tempers? I can hear the angry remarks that began to fly back and forth between Gramps and his visitors, as though I was right there in his office.

One of the Medleys was shouting at Gramps. "Lamport, we know the old lady had a fortune invested on your advice. She gave you that money in trust and it belongs to *us*. And we want it *now*!"

The other Medley's voice was even louder. "Whether you

like it or not, Lamport, we're entitled to that money under the will she *signed*. Never mind the changes she *thought* she wanted to make. Thinking's one thing; doing's another. What's done is done. So don't you go getting the notion you're gonna keep all that cash, y'hear?"

"You two haven't the foggiest idea what you're talking about," I heard Grandfather say. His voice was booming by this time. "Rebecca's money is safely tied up in bonds and land mortgages and there's hardly a penny in her trust account with my law office."

"You're lying, Ira," Priscilla Cranbrooke said, practically screaming. "Aunt Rebecca, bless her soul, meant us to have that money the moment she passed on!"

"These things can't happen overnight," my grandfather protested. "There are legal procedures that have to be followed. Can't you three get that through your heads? Or has common sense been entirely replaced by greed?"

"See, Lamport, there you go insulting us, Rebecca O'Hearn's own flesh and blood, and you're depriving us of our inheritance."

The other Medley took up where his brother left off. "Where I come from, Lamport, that's plain down-to-earth stealing. Theft! That's what it is. You're a thief!"

"And you're a pack of damn liars," Gramps shot back. "And I'll thank you to call me *Mister* Lamport from now on."

"There isn't gonna be any 'from now on'," Priscilla said.

At last the oak doors were thrust open. All were on their feet now. Dennis Medley was speaking, wagging an index finger menacingly in the direction of my grandfather. In a loud and angry voice he was saying, "Very well, Mr. Lamport, if you can't bring yourself to do your duty under the will, we'll find another lawyer who *can*!"

Without another word, the Medleys and their sister Priscilla filed out of the house, Harold Medley slamming the front door behind him.

Once the door was closed and they were presumably out of range, I heard my grandfather say in a loud voice, as though delivering a public proclamation, "Blessed are the greedy for they shall inherit the earth!"

Mondays, I learned, were traditionally the busiest days in the week for my grandfather. This was because the majority of local crimes were committed during the weekends, petty crimes mostly — drunkenness, minor assaults, careless driving, offences of that nature. Gramps said the reason was that people had too much time on their hands on Saturdays and Sundays. Before they knew it, they were on the wrong side of the law and standing in the dock before the judge in Port Sanford's courthouse on Monday morning.

This particular Monday morning was no exception to that rule. Immediately after his meeting with Mrs. O'Hearn's heirs, I heard Gramps inform his secretary that he was off to court to arrange bail for Harry Clydesdale. "Oh, no, not Harry again!" Miss Trimble said. "Yes," Grandfather said, "He had one beer too many, well, *ten* too many's more like it, Saturday night at the country club, got into a fight with his brother-in-law over their golf scores, and ended up practically wrecking the bar and half the furniture in the place. It'll be a miracle if he stays out of jail this time. I don't expect to be back here until later this afternoon. Got a dangerous driving case and one grievous assault, as well, coming up after lunch."

Before Grandfather departed for the courthouse, taking with him his heavily stuffed briefcase, he gave Miss Trimble some instructions about papers that had to be prepared in connection with Mrs. O'Hearn's estate. On his way out he said to his housekeeper, "Don't bother with lunch for me, Mrs.

Bjorklund, I'll probably only have time for a fast sandwich at the Kozy Korner downtown." Spotting me in the hallway, he called to Mrs. Bjorklund again, "By the way, Mrs. B., those butter tarts you're baking … Ben can have mine. Just make sure he saves me one or two." He gave me a wink, then strode out of the house, looking at his gold pocket watch as he made his way to the old Buick in the driveway.

I gave that wink of his a lot of thought for the rest of that Monday. Was it some kind of signpost informing me that he and I were about to head in a new direction? I certainly hoped so. A glance at the calendar made it very evident that Gramps and I were still facing the longest part of the summer together. If the days ahead were merely destined to be repetitions of the days gone by, then returning to school in September — which had never been my favourite event of the year in the past — would actually come as a treat.

# Nine

Shortly after my grandfather's departure for the Port Sanford courthouse, I heard my name called. "Ben, can you come here a moment, please?" It was Miss Trimble, summoning me to Gramps' office. I entered the front room through the sliding doors, which had been left wide open because Grandfather had not yet seen fit to invest in an air conditioner. There I found his secretary almost on her knees, making a desperate attempt to lift a carton that lay on the rug next to my grandfather's desk. "Can you help me with this, Ben?" Miss Trimble pleaded.

"Sure," I said, and bent to pick up the carton. It was large, without a lid, and I could see that it was crammed with papers, files and ledgers between thick covers. Heavy, too, but I was determined to prove to Miss Trimble that I could manage such a load without difficulty. To my embarrassment, my first attempt failed after I'd lifted the box no more than a few inches off the floor, and the carton landed on my toes, causing me to wince in pain (I was wearing sneakers at the time; steel-capped boots would have made more sense). I bent to try again. "Where'd you say you want this carton?" I asked Miss Trimble. "I need it on my desk, next to my typewriter, if that's possible," she replied. The woman had never so much as given me the time of day before this, I thought, but if I could oblige her by performing this task, perhaps she and I could get beyond "Good morning" and "Good evening" and actually have a conversation.

A second attempt also failed. But on the third try I gave a mighty heave upward and lurched forward, landing the carton at the desired spot as though it had just fallen from the roof of a thirty-storey skyscraper. Despite the clumsiness of my effort, Miss Trimble was impressed. "My, it's nice to have a strong young man about the house!" she said. "I would have asked your grandfather, but I don't think a man his age ought to be doing that sort of thing, you know." She pointed to the armchair near her desk. "Sit down and catch your breath, Ben," she said.

"I'm okay," I said. I stood for a moment, feeling awkward. Then, gathering up courage, I said, "Do you think my grandfather would mind if I look around his office a bit? I know there's a lot of private stuff here, but I'd just like to look at some of his books and pictures."

"I don't see why not," Miss Trimble said. "As a matter of fact, I think Mr. Lamport would be rather pleased. If you don't mind my saying so, Ben, your grandfather's been ... how shall I put it? ... Disappointed? Yes, I guess one could say disappointed."

"About what?"

"Well — " She seemed hesitant to continue.

"Please," I said, "I'd really like to know. Why's he disappointed?"

"To be honest about it, he's had the feeling you really don't want to be here, that you don't find him or what he does at all interesting. Perhaps if you take a good look around his office, you'll feel differently."

"That's funny," I said, "I've had the feeling that he's not

terribly interested in *me*. I think I know the reason. Once my mom grew up and left home, Gramps probably figured, Great! now he didn't have the headaches of being a parent, and he could concentrate on being a lawyer. Now I've showed up, and I guess in a way he feels as though he's got to be a parent all over again. It's a case of he's too old and I'm too young."

Miss Trimble was standing beside her desk, but showing no sign that she was eager to return to work. Something about the way she cocked her head, and the openness of her thin face, encouraged me to go on. "I think I made a bad choice," I said.

"What choice is that, Ben?"

"My parents offered to send me to a summer camp for July and August, a place down east called Camp Pinestone. The brochure looked terrific, as a matter of fact. You know, lots of sailing, canoeing, overnight trips, tuck shop, comfortable cabins. There was another camp too, down in Vermont, that looked great. My dad had gone there when he was a kid."

"Why didn't you take them up on their offer?"

"You want to know the truth?" Miss Trimble said of course she did. "Well, the truth was, I felt like they — I mean my mother and father — were really just looking for a way to ship me off somewhere, *any*where. I know it sounds stupid, but when you're an only child, like I am, and your folks have split, like mine did, well, no matter how much they offer you and give you, you feel sort of left out, like you're not entirely a part of their lives. So I told them if they could arrange for me to spend the summer here with Gramps I'd prefer it. After all, he *is* my closest relative. But I'm afraid I was wrong, and poor old Gramps probably couldn't find an excuse to get out of having me. So, here we are, Gramps and me, stuck with each other."

Miss Trimble's eyes fell for a moment to the watch on her left wrist, one of those sensible-looking timepieces I'd seen on nurses' wrists in hospitals. "Time for my morning break," she said. She reached for a Thermos jug behind her typewriter, then produced two drinking glasses. "I've made some iced tea," she said, then leaned toward me and said in a hushed tone, "but don't ever let on to Mrs. Bjorklund. Fact is, I like mine better than hers, so I bring my own from home. I assume one glassful won't stunt your growth, Ben."

We sat in silence for a few minutes, sipping our iced tea. At last she spoke up. "You're wrong … I mean about your grandfather. I happen to know that he was pleased — in fact flattered — when your mother approached him about your staying here with him. And if it hadn't been for this O'Hearn disaster — " Abruptly Miss Trimble covered her lips with both hands. "I'm sorry, Ben, please ignore what I just said."

I pretended I hadn't heard her request. "What disaster?" I asked putting down my glass of iced tea, gazing intently into the secretary's eyes.

Miss Trimble seemed taken aback by my sudden and intense interest. "No, no," she said quickly, almost as though she was out of breath, "I didn't mean to say 'disaster.' I don't know what on earth made me say it."

"People don't use a word like 'disaster' unless they mean it. What about the O'Hearn disaster, Miss Trimble?"

The woman's voice took an unexpected turn now, becoming firm, reminding me of a schoolteacher about to hand out a detention. "I'm afraid you'll have to excuse me, young man. I've a great deal of work to finish before Mr. Lamport's return this afternoon." She cast her eyes in the direction of the open oak doors. "Now if you don't mind — "

"Are you kicking me out of my grandfather's office?" I made my question sound as if I couldn't believe this was actually happening.

"No," she replied calmly. "It's not my place to do such a

thing. But it's also not my place to reveal client business. A lawyer's stock-in-trade is — "

"Yes, I know," I said, impatiently interrupting her. "I've already had Gramps' sermon about confidentiality, thank you."

"Well, then, I needn't belabour the point, need I? So you'll have to excuse me, Ben."

"You said a little while ago that my grandfather is disappointed because he thinks I'm not interested in him and what he does. Well, that's not true. He was very upset when old lady O'Hearn died ... upset with himself. Part of the trouble had to do with that dog of hers."

"He told you about what's going to happen to the dog?"

"Yes. But I have a hunch there's a lot more to the story. There is, isn't there, Miss Trimble?"

Grandfather's secretary pressed her thin lips together tightly, as though nothing short of a crowbar would pry them apart.

Forcing a smile so I wouldn't appear too obnoxious, I said, "It's no use, Miss Trimble. I've already proved that I'm stronger than you, so I'm not leaving and I don't like your chances of picking me up and throwing me out. So ... what's this about Gramps and the O'Hearn disaster?"

# Ten

**M**iss Trimble moved almost on tiptoes to the archway, satisfied herself that we were alone — Mrs. Bjorklund was nowhere to be seen — then returned to her desk, sat down and folded her hands on her knees.

"Now, then," she began slowly, speaking quietly, "do you know what a will is, Ben?"

"Yes," I said. "My grandfather has already explained how wills work and how important they are."

"Very well. In that case, perhaps you understand that Mrs. O'Hearn is ... I mean *was* ... a very wealthy and somewhat eccentric lady. In most situations she was a very decisive person. When it came to running her O'Hearn Estate, or going on transatlantic ocean cruises or travelling to different places in Europe or sitting on the boards of the local hospital and library, she was famous for making up her mind quickly and acting without hesitation. Unfortunately, when it came to making her will, the opposite was true.

"Part of the problem was that, having no children of her own, she was faced with the question whom to leave her millions to, and, believe me, that was not an easy question to resolve. Those three people you saw come in this morning — her niece and nephews — they're her only living relatives. It's no exaggeration to say Mrs. O'Hearn agonized constantly about leaving them the bulk of her fortune. At times she looked on them rather kindly; at other times she swore to your grandfather that she couldn't stand the sight or sound of them.

"So every few months, sure enough, she'd be on the phone to Mr. Lamport, or here at the office or summoning him to her estate, giving him instructions to prepare a new will.

"Well, back in May of this year — yes, just a couple of months or so ago — she had your grandfather draft up a new will. I guess she was in one of her rare 'family' moods. Maybe she loved her niece and nephews but I think more likely she was motivated at the time by pity, or perhaps by gratitude because they made a bit of a fuss over her ninetieth birthday, a dinner party and all. She signed a will leaving the biggest chunk by far of her money and property to the three of them. The rest of her fortune was to be divided among several of her favourite charities.

"Then, just a few days ago, I'm not sure how or why it happened, but she had a very big change of heart."

I said, "That would be the day Gramps and I were having lunch and you interrupted to say she was on the phone, and I thought Gramps was going to go right through the roof."

"Exactly. That afternoon, when you accompanied your grandfather to her house, she gave a whole new and different set of instructions to Mr. Lamport. The long and short of it was that she left everything the other way around, so to speak. In other words, eighty-five percent of everything she owned was to be divided equally among the Port Sanford Hospital, the local library, the local branches of the Salvation Army and Red Cross, and a conservatory down in Toronto where she took music lessons. At one time, when she was young, she had ambitions to be a concert pianist, you know. The remaining fifteen percent was to be divided equally among

Mrs. Cranbrooke and the two Medley brothers."

"But she never got around to signing the new will, right?" I said.

"Right," Miss Trimble said, a sad look on her face. "If only she'd managed to live another day, or even a few hours longer, the new will would have been signed, sealed and delivered, as they say."

"Is that considered a disaster?" I asked. "I've always thought of disasters as things you see in the papers or in the television newscasts … ships sinking, airplanes crashing, volcanoes erupting."

Miss Trimble took a moment to ponder the question. "Perhaps the word 'disaster' *is* a bit strong," she replied in that slow teacherly way she had of speaking. "But look at it from the standpoint of the charities that stood to benefit if she'd signed her new will. They'd have gotten millions of dollars that they urgently need to carry on their good work. Instead, they'll have to be content with much less, and the bulk of Mrs. O'Hearn's fortune will end up instead in three sets of hands that have never really done a day's work. And the worst part of it all — speaking for myself, Ben — is sitting here and listening to your grandfather blaming himself."

"What about the dog — Josh — how does *he* fit into this?" I said.

"The will she signed directed that Josh be put down as soon as possible after her death."

"But wasn't that a cruel thing to order Gramps to do?"

"Oh, no," Miss Trimble said quickly, "not at all. In Mrs. O'Hearn's mind that was the most *humane* thing to do. Josh is very old, he's been ailing on and off for the last year or so, and she figured the dog would be miserable once she was no longer around. Besides, the truth is that her precious relatives wouldn't have wanted to adopt Josh, and Mr. and Mrs. Tidy will probably retire to Florida or someplace down south once the estate is sold. They wouldn't be in a position to care for Josh."

"What about Gramps, then?" I suggested. "He lives all alone in this big spook-house. Josh would be company for him."

Miss Trimble smiled, but as before it was mostly sadness that I saw in her thin face. "Mr. Lamport's loved animals as long as I've know him — horses, dogs, farm animals — but there's no way he would fail to carry out his client's instructions. No, Ben, having to kill that little dog is killing your grandfather. But I know him. He'll do his duty."

Lowering her voice, and leaning forward as if to impart a confidence, Miss Trimble added, "There's another reason Ira — I mean Mr. Lamport — couldn't keep the dog here: Mrs. Bjorklund would quit the moment that poor little beast set foot — or perhaps I should say all four feet — in this house. She hates animals, especially dogs. Doesn't like the mess they make, the noises they make. In fact, if it weren't for Mrs. Bjorklund — "

Suddenly Miss Trimble halted. She glanced anxiously toward the hall beyond the archway from where the sound of retreating footsteps could be heard, causing the old oak floorboards there to groan.

"Mrs. Bjorklund?" Grandfather's secretary called out, rising nervously from her chair, her hands pressed together, looking tense. "Mrs. Bjorklund, are you there?"

The footsteps faded. Nothing but total silence now. Not a peep from any other part of the house, except for the tick-tock of the hall clock.

For a moment we exchanged puzzled looks, Miss Trimble and I. Then her face took on a look of fear. "I thought she was busy upstairs," Miss Trimble said. Sounding deeply upset, she called out once again, "Mrs. Bjorklund?"

Again there was no reply. Mrs. Bjorklund had stationed herself just outside the office but out of our sight. She had been eavesdropping and must have overheard the entire account concerning the O'Hearn "disaster."

Miss Trimble sank into her chair. She was pale and wringing her bony hands between which a lace handkerchief was scrunched. Looking up at me she said in a hoarse whisper, "My God, Ben, what have I gone and done?"

# Eleven

Foul. That's the word that springs to mind to describe Grandfather's mood when he returned from court that day. By the scowl on his face as he emerged from his car, lumbered up the porch steps and entered the house slamming the front door behind him, I detected that things had not gone well for him downtown at the old stone courthouse. "Hi, Gramps," I called out. Without acknowledging my greeting he strode past me into his office. My eyes followed him and I watched as he flung his battered briefcase down as though it was a sack of potatoes.

"Are you all right?" I heard Miss Trimble inquire, her voice soft, as though she feared that even this innocent question might add to my grandfather's obvious unhappiness. At first Grandfather ignored her question. "Mr. Lamport?" she said in her hesitant way, "I asked if you're all right."

Through the broad open archway leading into his office I could see my grandfather standing in the middle of the room. His back was to me but I could tell that his head was bent. His shoulders drooped and his arms hung at his sides. I would have said he looked lifeless just then, except that his hands were clenched into tight fists. At last he spoke. "I don't know what's gone wrong with me," he said, so quietly that he seemed to be talking to himself and not to his secretary. "Three cases in court today and every one of 'em a loser. They've imported this young prosecutor from Toronto, some hotshot fresh out of law school. I took one look at this kid and figured for sure he was still in diapers. And what happens? This 'kid' rolls over me like a bull-dozer. Harry Clydesdale's bail application was refused by the judge and he's got to stay put in the clink until his trial next month. Lost my dangerous driving case. And my client — the one charged with grievous assault — ended up getting six months in jail and a thousand dollar fine."

"Well, now, Mr. Lamport, what is it you always say? 'You can't win 'em all.'" Miss Trimble put on her most cheerful tone. "Tomorrow is another day. I'm sure things'll look rosier in the morning."

"No, Agnes, I'm afraid not. I'm losing my touch, and that's a fact."

"Oh, nonsense!" Miss Trimble said. "I've worked for you for more years than either of us cares to remember, and this is the first time I've heard you feel sorry for yourself. You'll teach this young upstart at the courthouse a thing or two, just you wait and see."

Grandfather walked slowly over to his desk and sat down in his high-back chair. "I'm like Mrs. O'Hearn's dog, Josh. Old. Long past my prime. Becoming useless. That's why this youngster ran circles around me today in court. He could sense I was over the hill, tired out. He could smell old age a mile away, Agnes."

"Shame on you, Ira Lamport," Miss Trimble chided. "Imagine! Comparing yourself to a … a dog, of all things."

"Truth is," Grandfather said, "that mutt and I seem to have an awful lot in common. I look at that little runt — still yap-ping away when half the time he doesn't even know what he's yapping about — and I see myself. I look at that animal who's about to be destroyed, and I see myself. But somehow it's not right, Agnes, it's not right at all."

"What's not right?"

"That dog still has life in him, flesh and blood and a heart that beats, just as I have. Even if I *am* over the hill, I'm not ready to die. Why should *he*? Why should Josh have to die? I never should have agreed to carry out Rebecca O'Hearn's instructions. I should've argued with the old tyrant. I should've had the courage, and the decency, to say 'No, Rebecca, you're wrong, and I won't do it, I won't kill your dog.'"

"My God, Mr. Lamport, you're making a mountain out of a molehill. Anyway, you'll be interested to know your grandson paid me a visit. Well, actually I needed a stronger back than mine to hoist that box. I must say he was very helpful. Besides, he seemed genuinely interested in looking around your office, examining some of your books and pictures. And the two of us had a very nice chat. He's a determined young man, likes to get to the bottom of things. I think he might make a fine lawyer himself some day. A sort of chip off the old block, as they say."

"He says he'd rather be an airline pilot," my grandfather said, with a faint chuckle. "I'm beginning to think the kid's got more sense than I did when I was his age. I was about twelve years old when I announced to my folks that I wanted to be a lawyer and not a farmer. The way things have been going lately, I wish I could go back in time and change that decision."

"Well, I for one am very glad you can't go back," said Miss Trimble firmly. "Just imagine, if you hadn't become a lawyer I wouldn't have this job, would I? I probably would have ended up in some humdrum line of work, like working as a clerk in my father's insurance agency. You knew my father very well, Mr. Lamport, so you can picture what a bowl of cherries my life would have been, slaving away day and night for dear Delmore Trimble. Anyway, in my opinion Ben Marshall could do a lot worse than follow in his grandfather's footsteps. I just think it's a pity that the two of you — " Grandfather's secretary put a hand to her lips, silencing herself.

"Go on," Gramps said gruffly. "Finish what you were going to say. You think it's a pity that the two of us *what*?"

"I — uh — I'm sorry," Miss Trimble stammered, "really, it's none of my business. I mean, I've no right to go poking my nose into your private family affairs."

"Good God, woman," Gramps said, "out with it! It's a pity that *what*?"

Miss Trimble took a deep breath, then spoke quickly, as though preparing to make a hasty retreat the moment her words landed in Gramps' ears. "It's a pity that you think he's not interested in you, and *he* thinks you're not interested in *him*."

His voice rising, Grandfather said, "Is that what my grandson told you … that I'm not interested in him? What on earth were the two of you doing while I was at the courthouse, staging some kind of a … a soap opera? Was he telling you his life story, was that it?"

"No, no, honestly — "

"Telling you how abandoned he feels because his mother's gallivanting all over the planet and his father's got his doctorly nose stuck in a row of sutures? Talk about feeling sorry for one's self! That kid has no idea how lucky he is. A solid roof over his head, three square meals a day. A brand new two-wheeler. Money in his pocket. A whole summer off. What more could any thirteen-year-old ask?"

From where I was sitting at the bottom of the flight of steps that led to the second storey, I heard my grandfather call out to me. "Ben!" At first I didn't respond. His tone was harsh as he repeated, "Ben!"

I got up. "Yes," I said.

"Come here, boy."

There must have been an invisible hand that prodded me

into Grandfather's office for I certainly had no wish to enter that room of my own free will. My grandfather was standing behind his desk, peering across the room at me. Nervously, I glanced to my right, hoping for some expression of moral support from Miss Trimble during the storm which was surely about to break, but Grandfather's secretary seemed to have shrivelled up and she offered me nothing but a look of extreme discomfort, underlined by the biting of her bottom lip.

"It appears, young man, that you've unburdened yourself of all your worldly sorrows — your *supposed* worldly sorrows, is more like it — to Miss Trimble here during my absence today. Apparently you feel neglected by me — "

Miss Trimble spoke up. "Oh, no, I didn't say that, not at all, Mr. Lamport!"

Without taking his eyes from me Grandfather said, "*I'll* handle this, Miss Trimble, thank you." My grandfather's face took on a stony look. His eyes narrowed almost to slits the way lawyers' eyes do when they're cross-examining hostile witnesses. Maintaining his position behind his desk, he began questioning me, his voice quietly cold, his manner distant yet menacing, as though *I* were a hostile witness. "I want the truth, young man," he said. "You occupy a clean spacious room of your own in this house, do you not?"

"Yes."

"And the meals here, are they not plentiful and nourishing?"

"They are."

"Has anyone imposed any restrictions on your freedom or made any unreasonable demands on your time?"

"No, sir."

"Your privacy has been respected, has it not?"

"Yes, sir."

"Is it a fair assumption, then, that the standard of hospitality exhibited in this household affords a degree of comfort and security that any boy in his right mind should accept with gratitude?"

I gulped and said, "Would you mind repeating that last question? I'm afraid I didn't manage to catch all the words."

"Don't toy with me, young man," Grandfather shot back. "I'm sure you're bright enough to have understood what I asked."

"I wish you'd stop calling me 'young man'," I said. "All it does is confuse me because I don't feel young and I don't feel like a man. I feel like I'm something in between, but I'm not sure what exactly."

"Let's not get bogged down with semantics," Grandfather said.

"With what? What's semantics?"

"Language. Let's not play around with words. Answer the question: Are we not meeting your expectations here?"

"No, I'm afraid not. In fact, like I told Miss Trimble, I think I made a huge mistake coming here instead of going to summer camp. I get the feeling that you're blaming me as well as yourself for this whole mess."

"Whole mess? What whole mess? What're you talking about?"

"You know what I'm talking about," I said. "Miss Trimble calls it the O'Hearn disaster."

I happened to catch sight of Miss Trimble out of the corner of my eye. At the words "the O'Hearn disaster" she shifted forward uneasily in her secretarial chair, sitting now on the edge of the seat. She looked up at me with a pleading expression. But Grandfather, with a look of disbelief and disappointment in his eyes, raised his hands, silencing her. "Agnes?" He paused. "Agnes, am I correct in assuming that you took the liberty of discussing the O'Hearn matter with my grandson, yes or no?" My grandfather put this question to Miss Trimble quietly, but the "yes or no" left no doubt that behind the soft tone of voice there was a barely controlled fury.

Before Miss Trimble could reply, I said, "It's not her

fault. I pried it out of her."

Still fixing his gaze on his secretary, Grandfather said to me, "Pried *what* out of her?"

"That you were too late getting to Mrs. O'Hearn with the new will, which means a lot of deserving people are going to lose out on millions of dollars."

"That's not quite the way I put it," Miss Trimble said, choking back tears now. "Please, Mr. Lamport, let me explain."

"There's nothing to explain," my grandfather said coldly, glaring at his secretary, seemingly without pity despite the look of misery on her face. "All these years you've worked here as my secretary, Agnes ... all these years of loyalty, and discretion, and sound judgement ... and suddenly you toss all these virtues into the wind and your only excuse is that some thirteen-year-old who had no business poking his nose into my office in the first place — "

"I wasn't 'poking my nose' into your precious office," I shouted. "Miss Trimble needed help to lift that carton of papers."

Grandfather gave me a withering look. "When I want your account of this shabby affair I'll ask for it. Until then, have the decency to do something that obviously doesn't come easily to you, Ben: Keep quiet!"

Turning his attention once again to his unhappy secretary, my grandfather said, "Agnes, you know how gossip travels from mouth to mouth in this town. It spreads faster than mustard on a hot dog. I trust these disclosures haven't reached any other ears around here."

There was an awkward silence. Miss Trimble and I exchanged anxious glances.

"Well," Gramps demanded impatiently, "at least assure me that whatever you two discussed hasn't gone beyond the four walls of this office."

Miss Trimble straightened herself, took a deep breath, as

though filling her lungs with courage, then looked my grandfather straight in the eye. "We think Mrs. Bjorklund overheard
our conversation, Mr. Lamport."

Trying desperately now to come to the secretary's aid, I
added quickly, "Eavesdropping, that's what she was doing. We
had no idea she was just outside the office doors until we heard
her footsteps — "

"As she stole away," Miss Trimble said, finishing my sentence.

My grandfather let out a deep groan.

"But maybe that's not a bad thing," I said to Grandfather.
"After all, she hardly ever talks to anybody, as far as I can tell."

Grandfather's head shook slowly from side to side. I'd obviously failed to convince him. "People who eavesdrop always end
up spilling whatever their little ears have heard, I guarantee it,"
he said. "By this time tomorrow the word'll be on the street from
one end of Port Sanford to the other. 'Ira Lamport, old Ira, yessir,
he's blown it, he's really gone and blown it.' I can hear it all now."

Grandfather turned his back on us. "Agnes," he said, his
voice quiet again, "I think you'd better go home. Stay home
tomorrow, then come to see me the day after."

"Are you firing me? Is that what you're trying to tell me
... that I'm dismissed?"

There was no reply from Grandfather, and his silence
made it all the worse for Miss Trimble. Without another
word, but shooting a look at me that seemed to say "Ben
Marshall, how could you do this to me?" my grandfather's secretary gathered up her purse and dashed from the room.

At that moment, it struck me that all three of us — my
grandfather, his secretary and I — were sharing the same
regret. All three of us wished I had never chosen to spend this
summer in Port Sanford.

# Twelve

**B**reakfast next morning, not surprisingly, was a solemn affair. Mrs. Bjorklund managed her customary unsmiling "Good morning" and served up scrambled eggs and hot biscuits which Grandfather and I barely touched. Every few minutes my grandfather would glance at his old-fashioned gold pocket watch. He seemed nervous, as though expecting the arrival of a client any moment. From time to time he looked over his shoulder in the direction of the front door, muttering to himself about how it was getting late.

When at last there was a sharp ring of the doorbell, my grandfather rose from his seat at the dining-room table with a start. "I'll get the door," he called to Mrs. Bjorklund, who was in the kitchen. There was an air of determination about the way he strode to the front door.

I heard a woman say, "Good morning, Mr. Lamport," and recognized the voice of Hilda Tidy. Her greeting was immediately punctuated by an ear-piercing bark and, as she entered the front hall, I saw that in her plump arms she held Mrs. O'Hearn's Chihuahua, Josh. Spotting me, Mrs. Tidy called out, "Good morning, Ben." She set the dog down on the floor. "Josh," she said softly, "go say hello to your friend Ben. There's a good boy."

I left the dining-room table intending to join the others but Josh, barking steadily now in that shrill yap of his, made it very clear that three was company but four a crowd.

"Shame on you, Josh," Mrs. Tidy chided. "Ben loves you, you silly old creature." She scooped up the tiny animal as if he weighed no more than a feather. "There there, Josh, *every-body* loves you, so stop all that racket, y'hear?"

The dog eyed me suspiciously but, safely enfolded in the woman's generous arms, fell silent. Mrs. Tidy said to Grandfather, "Are you sure you don't want me to come with you this morning? It might make things a bit easier for you."

"Thank you, no," Grandfather said. "I've made the appointment with Doc Hetherington for ten o'clock. I understand these things don't take too long. Anyway, I'd best handle this alone, Mrs. Tidy."

There was a long pause during which none of us spoke. Mrs. Tidy continued cradling Josh in her arms, rocking him gently as if he were a baby. Then, very slowly, she set the dog down on the floor once again. She gazed intently at my grandfather. "You're absolutely sure about this, Ira?"

A sad smile lifted the corners of Grandfather's mouth. Looking down at the dog, he said, "Yes. Thank you for your concern, Hilda."

"In that case," the woman said, her voice catching in her throat, "I'll be on my way. There's a hundred and one things to do back at the estate before it goes up for sale."

"Yes, of course," Grandfather agreed.

Mrs. Tidy bent down, and stroked Josh's head behind his ears. "Bye, Josh, ol' darlin'. See you in heaven."

She turned and left quickly, not looking back. Josh made no move to follow after her. He simply stood there in the middle of the entrance hall next to Gramps, looking somehow smaller than before.

I broke the stillness, asking, "Gramps, are you really taking him to the vet?"

"Yes."

"When?"

"Now."

"But it's not even nine o'clock. I heard you say the appointment's for ten."

"That's right."

"What's the rush, then?"

"There's no rush. I just want to get this over and done. I figure the sooner I get to Doctor Hetherington's the sooner — " Grandfather couldn't bring himself to finish.

"What would happen if you decided at the last minute not to go through with this?" I asked.

Grandfather shook his head. "That would be the thin edge of the wedge, boy. You disobey one direction from a client, next thing you know you're disobeying others for no reason other than you don't like having to carry out orders. That's no way to run a law practice. It's sure as heck not Ira Lamport's way to run a law practice."

"Do you suppose we could at least give Josh a cookie, maybe a drink, too? He sort of looks like he's wasting away." Incredibly, the dog seemed to be shrinking even as I stood looking down at him.

"You mean, the way they give a condemned prisoner a last meal?"

"Well, sort of like that," I said.

The grandfather clock in the hall suddenly came to life, its loud chimes announcing nine o'clock. "I guess another couple of minutes won't matter," Gramps said. He called to Mrs. Bjorklund to fetch one of Mrs. Tidy's shortbread cookies from the small tin she'd given us a few days earlier. Grandfather's housekeeper set the cookie down on the floor, making sure not to get too close to the Chihuahua, a look of disapproval on her stern face. I could tell what was on the woman's mind: crumbs all over her spotless hardwood floor and the necessity to go over it once again with a mop.

Gramps and I looked on as Josh devoured the shortbread. There were crumbs, lots of them, and Josh was determined not to overlook so much as a single tidbit.

When finally the last microscopic crumb had been lapped up, I said, "Do you want me to come with you, Gramps? I can hold him while you drive."

Gramps reached for a hat that hung on one of the ornate brass hooks next to the hall mirror. Without looking at me, he said, "No, Ben, you'd better stay here. This is something I've got to do by myself."

I took a step toward him. "But I'd like to, honest."

"The answer's no, boy. Now please, don't give me a hard time, not this morning of all mornings. Understand?"

"But *why* can't I just go to the vet with you?" I demanded.

"I am *not* accustomed to being cross-examined," Grandfather said. "No is a simple two-letter word, Ben, and it means no."

I persisted. "But you haven't explained why."

"Why? Because you're too young, that's one reason. Because I've had the experience of seeing animals put down and it's not a pretty sight, that's another reason. How many more do you need for God's sake?"

"In other words," I said with a look of disgust, "you're flip-flopping."

"Flip-flopping? What's that supposed to mean?"

"It means one day you say one thing, next day you turn around and say the very opposite."

"I swear, Ben, I don't know what you're talking about." Grandfather began rattling the car keys in his hand impatiently.

"You remember what you told me the night we pulled up

in front of Mrs. O'Hearn's?" I was shouting now. "You said death and dying are as much part of life as eating and sleeping. Those were your very words. You said I might as well find out now, that it's part of my education. Remember? Now you're telling me something completely different. A flip-flopper, that's what you are!"

My grandfather's mouth opened wide and I expected an angry torrent of rebuke. Instead — silence. He must have been counting to ten, or maybe twenty, or maybe a hundred, giving himself time to get his temper under control. When finally he was able to speak, the words were delivered in a surprisingly even tone. "Listen to me, Ben," he said. "This business with the dog, it's one of the ugliest things I've ever had to do. In fact, it's the ugliest. For the first time in all my years of being a lawyer I'm ashamed of what I have to do. And I don't want you to be a part of this. I repeat: I do *not* want you involved in this."

I turned away. Without looking at my grandfather, I said, "Well, that's just great. Three strikes and I'm out."

"Meaning? — "

"Meaning I'm not part of my mother's life; I'm not part of my father's life; and I'm sure as heck not part of *your* life."

When I turned to face him, after saying this, I added, "You know something, Gramps? You've got more feeling for that dog than you have for your own grandson."

"That's not true, Ben. That's a nasty accusation. I feel rotten enough about the way things are turning out these days without you making things worse. Instead of feeling so sorry for yourself, you might try feeling at least a *little* sorry for me. I'm the one who's suffering here, you know."

"I know that," I said. "You sure haven't kept it a secret. All I want to do is keep you company. Is that so terrible?"

There was another long silence, only this time I didn't imagine my grandfather was counting numbers. "There's no doubt about it, boy. You've inherited the worst qualities of your mother and father. You're brazen like her. And you've a one-track mind like him."

"That's funny," I said. "Whenever my folks think I'm being a pain in the neck, they tell me I remind them of you."

"In that case," Gramps said, his voice resuming its firmness, "you carry Josh out to the car. I think cars make him nervous, so you better hold on to him, make him comfortable, poor little devil."

The Hetherington Animal Clinic was on McDougall Avenue, a side street just off Port Sanford's main street. In the early 1900s, the more prosperous folks in the region settled on this street, building spacious two-storey red brick houses near the main thoroughfare. It made sense then, living close to where the stores were located, being able to shop for groceries and hardware and yard goods without having to hitch up the horse and buggy and travel for miles over crude dirt roads.

Except for a bit of trim here or a patch of paint there, the houses on McDougall all looked alike, standing alongside one another like a family of old cousins. Old and close, but not necessarily happy. Their lines were straight and severe. The panes of glass in their oversize front doors were frosted or stained and uninviting. Missing was the friendly white gingerbread that graced the stone houses in the outlying areas. From these homes on McDougall, many years ago, their inhabitants must have marched stiffly off to church Sunday mornings starched from head to toe, then marched stiffly home at noon for roast beef and Yorkshire pudding.

What a perfect spot, I thought, for Dr. Bryce Hetherington, the only veterinary surgeon in town, to operate a house of death for creatures like Josh.

Obeying a small sign that instructed us to ring and walk in, we entered by a side door, down a narrow flight of steps, through a windowless corridor and into a bare basement waiting room. Nothing relieved the monotony of the white-washed walls but a calendar from the Port Sanford Feed and Seed Company, showing a photograph of a solitary brown cow looking either incredibly content or incredibly bored. It was hard to tell which.

We stood, Grandfather and I, in silence. From an inner room, behind a closed door with a "Private" plaque, we could hear voices. "I guess the doc had a patient ahead of us," Grandfather said, and he glanced at his watch and gave a quiet sigh, as though he couldn't wait to get this mission over and done with.

I held Josh in my arms. His body felt warm against my thin cotton shirt. From time to time, as the voices from the adjoining room rose, Josh would utter a low growl. "I bet there's another dog in there," I said, noting the tension in Josh's limbs and the way his ears stood up and his nostrils flared catching vibrations or scents too subtle for mere humans. "Take it easy, old fella," I whispered, stroking his back.

Five minutes passed — five minutes which seemed to take forever — then the door marked "Private" opened. Out walked a young woman, smiling, holding a leash at the end of which a large Irish setter strained, its long feathery tail swinging wildly. The young woman was calling over her shoulder, "Thank you, Dr. Hetherington," when the setter and Josh caught sight of each other. Yapping his head off, Josh made a desperate attempt to free himself.

"There, there, Prince," the woman said, bending down and patting her dog's head soothingly. "It's only an itty-bitty Chihuahua." Looking up at me, she said in a pleasant voice, "What's your dog's name?"

"Josh," I replied.

"Well, Mr. Chihuahua," the woman said, addressing Josh

directly, "big things sure come in small packages! I wish Prince here had your gumption. You'll have to come over to our house and teach Prince how to be a *real* watchdog." Carefully she brought the back of her hand up to Josh's snout, waiting for him to sniff and satisfy himself that she was on his side, then giggled as he licked her hand approvingly. "See you, Josh," she said, and called over her shoulder again, "Thank you, Dr. Hetherington," as she departed.

"Come right in, gentlemen," said Dr. Hetherington, appearing in the doorway.

To my dismay, the doctor looked as though he'd been built by the same people who once upon a time had built the house he now occupied. He too was tall and very erect. He wore a white cotton jacket that was so crisp and starched that I imagined it could stand by itself when he took it off. A few strands of silvery hair spanned his scalp just above his high forehead. His complexion was the colour of old plaster. I was sure that if the man ever laughed, his face would crack, revealing an underlayer of lath.

Nodding in my direction, Dr. Hetherington said, "So this is your grandson Josh, Ira. Well, how-do-you-do, Josh." Dr. Hetherington's voice — despite his closeness — sounded hollow, as though it was coming from the far end of a long tunnel.

"My name's Ben," I said. "The *dog* is Josh."

To my surprise, Dr. Hetherington smiled and his face did not crack. "Good thing you straightened me out on that point," he said to me. "Otherwise I might've put the wrong patient to sleep, eh?" Giving me a wink, the doctor added, "Hope you don't mind a little joke, son. Moments like this, we have to keep our spirits up, don't we? Anyway, we're old friends, Josh and me. I've seen this little fella through everything from an upset stomach to a bout of pneumonia. One time years ago Rebecca called me, must've been midnight — "

Grandfather coughed louder than was necessary. "Doc, if you don't mind," he said, "perhaps we can get on with this. Ben's never been present at … well, you catch my drift, I'm sure."

Without a word, Dr Hetherington led us into his examining room and we gathered around a table that stood dead centre. An air conditioner, humming and rattling in one of the narrow casement windows, sent a chilly draft deflecting off the white walls and ceiling of the room into our faces. "I hope you don't find it too cool," the doctor said, noting that I'd given a slight shrug of my shoulders. "Summertime it can get pretty stuffy in here what with all the animals that come and go in a typical day. I'll never forget August two years ago, during the heat wave — "

Once again my grandfather was driven to cough almost violently. I'll say this much for Dr. Hetherington, he could take a hint. Cutting short what promised to be a lengthy anecdote about the heat wave, he said to me, speaking quietly but in that strangely hollow voice of his, "Ben, place Josh down here on the table and lie him on his side. I suggest you do it slowly and gently. We don't want to get the little fella excited or upset."

I did as the doctor instructed, relieved that so far there was no sign of resistance from Josh.

From a nearby cabinet, the doctor removed a hypodermic needle no larger than the kind my own doctor used the last time I received a polio shot. "The needle contains a dose — well, actually an overdose — of barbiturate," he explained, holding the tip up. I must have grimaced instinctively at the sight of the needle, and Dr. Hetherington did his best to reassure me. "If all goes well, it will act quickly. Now then," he went on, "Ira, while Ben sees to it that Josh lies as still as possible, please grip the toe of the dog's right foot and extend the leg as fully as you can."

This next step was accomplished again without resistance from Josh.

"We're doing fine, gentlemen, just fine," said Dr. Hetherington, adjusting his tortoise-shell framed eyeglasses so they sat almost at the tip of his nose. Bending closely over Josh now, Dr. Hetherington said quietly, "You know, miniature breeds like Chihuahuas always present a bit of a problem. Ah, yes, there we have it. Good." He was peering down at the upper part of Josh's front leg, just above the elbow. "Tricky things, these small veins."

The hypodermic needle at the ready in his hand, Dr. Hetherington spoke calmly. "Ira, would you kindly continue to hold Josh's leg fully extended with your left hand. Now pinch off that vein with your right hand. Try to keep the vein as prominent as possible so it's accessible, if you know what I mean."

I looked at Grandfather's face. Despite the coolness being thrust at us from the air conditioner, a fine film of perspiration dampened my grandfather's brow. His lips, pressed tightly together, were twitching ever so slightly. "Is this satisfactory, Bryce?" he asked, in an unsteady voice.

"Yes, indeed," the doctor replied. "Sorry I have to put you through this," he said to us, "but unlike my big-city counterparts, I don't have the luxury of a full-time assistant here at the clinic, only a part-timer who helps me when I'm attending larger farm animals. Now, then, if everyone will keep the dog in a steady position — "

The doctor's hand, his needle poised for the injection and his thumb resting on the plunger, moved slowly and carefully down until it was only an inch from the vein.

A cold sweat had turned my shirt clammy. My hands, which had been resting firmly but gently on Josh's torso, began to shake noticeably.

"Don't worry, Ben," said the doctor, "the barbiturate works swiftly."

"Will he feel any pain?" I asked.

"Not really. Usually they heave a deep sigh, give one final inhalation and they're off to sleep. Simple as that."

The needle's tip was almost touching the vein now. "By the way," Dr. Hetherington said, not looking up, "I overlooked having you sign the routine consent form, Ira. We can attend to that formality after. I assume we can proceed?"

There was no reply.

Still hovering over the dog's vein with the hypodermic, the doctor said, "Ira? Okay to go ahead?"

My grandfather seemed to have been struck speechless.

"Gramps," I said quietly, "can we get this over with, *please*?"

Sounding a bit impatient, Dr. Hetherington said, "Just say yes, Ira, because you can't expect a dog to lie perfectly still like this forever."

I saw grandfather's fingers suddenly relax their grip on Josh's leg. Then he removed his hand altogether and straightened himself. In a raspy voice, he said, "No."

"I beg your pardon?" the doctor said, holding the needle back in the air.

"I said no, Bryce."

"Meaning you want to put it off? Well, that's up to you of course, Ira. We can schedule another appointment later this week."

"We won't need another appointment, Doc. Not this week. Not ever."

The old veterinarian seemed taken aback. He began apologetically. "Is it something I said or did? Like I said, small dogs are not as easy to deal with in these situations because their veins — "

Grandfather raised a hand to stop the doctor. "It's got nothing to do with you, Doc. The trouble's with me. I can't explain it right now. Just tell me how much I owe you and we'll waste no more of your time."

Mrs. Bjorklund was sweeping the front porch as we pulled into the driveway. She put down her broom and advanced to the front step, a broad smile lighting up her face. Grandfather was first out of the car. "I've got some nice fresh coffee on the stove, Mr. Lamport," she called out. I'd never before seen the woman in such a bubbly mood.

Then I opened the front door on the passenger side.

Out jumped Josh.

He stretched himself to his full length, his four small legs splaying into the gravel. As though shedding the memory of the past hour, he shook himself thoroughly. Then from somewhere inside his soul came a series of high-pitched, cantankerous, ear-piercing barks. I broke into a laugh. Grandfather's housekeeper, however, found nothing funny or heart-warming about the dog's reappearance. Her face instantly froze into a stony mask. Promptly turning on her heels, she retreated into the house, the firmness of her chin and the stiffness of her neck making it clear that no four-legged guest would ever fit into her vision of good housekeeping.

As for Gramps, his reaction to Josh's latest declaration of independence was a weak smile, a smile that told me that sparing Josh's life had not really solved my grandfather's troubles. Far from it.

# Thirteen

There was a convenience store a couple of blocks from my grandfather's house. The owner, Mr. Dunsford, was a short man with a pot-belly and looked as though he sampled too many of the snacks he kept for sale. When I presented myself that morning and ordered two cans of dog food, Dunsford's eyebrows almost touched the ceiling.

"Don't tell me Ira Lamport has broken down finally and got himself a dog? Well, high time, I'd say. No man living alone should be without some kind of household companion. You sure two cans are enough?"

I wasn't about to set Mr. Dunsford straight. Besides, I wasn't sure myself whether or not Josh's residence at Grandfather's house was temporary. Once out of the car and into the house, Josh had been handed over to me with not a single word of advice or instruction. "Here, Ben, take him and see to his needs," was all Gramps said.

"Two cans doesn't sound like much for a dog, son," Dunsford said. "What did Ira get? A German shepherd, I bet. Or maybe one of them collies. A man Ira's size usually goes for a man-size dog." Dunsford punctuated this opinion with a self-confident smile, as though satisfied with his own worldly wisdom. How could I deflate him by pointing out how dead wrong he was? "This dog's got a very large personality," I said. "I'm not too sure that his appetite matches his personality, so we'll stick with two cans, thank you."

"Fine," said Mr. Dunsford, sliding the two cans of dog food across the counter, and accepting my cash. "But I know your grandfather. He loves a bargain. So you tell him it's a lot cheaper if he buys it from now on by the case. There's twelve cans to a case, y'know. And next time you come by, son, bring the dog along … that is, if he's not too big a handful for a young fella like you." Dunsford chuckled and handed me a free lollipop, giving me the feeling for a moment that I was still in diapers. "No, thanks," I said, declining the offer, "I'm gonna need *both* hands free to handle the dog." I hoped my sarcasm wasn't wasted on Dunsford. He laughed and said, "Well, next time then."

I spent much of the rest of that morning and afternoon alone, with only Josh to keep me company. Gramps chose to skip lunch, pleading that he had some legal emergency or other that needed his full attention. Agnes Trimble of course hadn't shown up for work. Frankly, her absence for the day was a good thing as far as I was concerned, for I was still bearing a heavy burden of guilt over what had happened to poor Agnes the day before.

By mid-afternoon Josh accepted my invitation to go for a walk. He wore a collar, but didn't come with a leash. Josh had been trained to heel, and he left my side only to do what a dog has to do, sniffing, lifting his hind leg, sniffing, lifting, sniffing, lifting. There wasn't a tree along our route that Josh didn't stop at, circling the base, sniffing the earth around it like a detective searching for clues, and leaving a drop or two to soak into the lowest patch of bark.

Gramps spent the rest of that afternoon closeted in his office, emerging only long enough to reject the lunch that Mrs. Bjorklund had prepared and, later, dinner.

At bedtime, I called out to him, "Good night, I'm taking Josh up with me, see you in the morning." From behind the closed doors of his office his muffled voice called back gruffly, "G'night."

I knew it was eleven o'clock when I heard the soft knock on my bedroom door because the chimes sent their mournful toll from the body of the grandfather's clock all the way up the broad staircase and throughout the second storey of the house. Blinking, seeing nothing in the darkness, I called out, "Who's there?" I heard Josh, who'd been asleep on the carpet beside my bed, rustle himself awake.

"It's me, Ben. You awake?"

"I am now." What did Gramps think, that I always talked in my sleep? Of course I was awake.

"I need to talk to you, Ben."

"Come in," I said, and sat up, rubbing my eyes and then switching on the lamp on my nighttable.

Grandfather opened the door, but remained in the doorway, one hand on the knob. The light from my lamp was weak, so that what I was staring at was a shadowy figure. "What's up?" I asked.

"I want you to pack your things, Ben. Right away, please. The sooner we get going the better."

I sat up straighter in bed, trying to put my thoughts together, trying to figure out what was happening. Was this Grandfather's way of getting rid of me? Had he spent the better part of this day wrestling with his conscience and come to the conclusion that I was the source of all the things that seemed to be going wrong? Here I was beginning to believe that he and I were finally learning to get along with one another and now ... now, was he calling an abrupt halt to the process? And if he was, why had he chosen to do so in practically the middle of the night?

Couldn't this have waited at least until tomorrow's sunrise?

I swung myself out of bed. "Okay," I said quietly, "give me a few minutes to throw my stuff together."

"I'll be waiting for you downstairs," Grandfather said. There was a flatness, a coldness, to his voice that warned me I'd better not take long to do as he ordered.

Clutching my suitcase with one hand, and an athletic bag with the other, I presented myself in the front hall to find Grandfather standing there, checking the time. "Hope I didn't keep you waiting," I said.

"Where's Josh?" Grandfather wanted to know, looking about him.

"Huh?"

"I said, where's Josh?"

"Why do we need Josh? You're just gonna drive me back to Toronto, right?"

"Whoever told you that?"

I shrugged. "Well, I assumed that's what you're about to do. Where else would we be going this time of night?"

"That's the trouble with young people nowadays," Gramps said grumpily. "You assume too much. *Think* more, and assume less."

"Well, thank you," I said, irritation rising up from my chest, "but couldn't this lecture have waited until breakfast in the morning?"

Checking the time on the clock once again, Grandfather mumbled, "Never put off till tomorrow what you can accomplish today."

"Okay, then," I said, trying desperately to piece my way through the mystery of the moment, "just where *are* we going, and what *are* we doing?"

"Time's wasting," my grandfather said. "Go fetch Josh. We're hitting the road."

We left the house without another word spoken, Grandfather making certain the front door was securely locked. The night sky was cloudless and there was just enough moonlight to give our exit from the house the appearance of an escape from prison, the two of us making our way along the driveway and into the Buick in absolute silence. Josh followed closely, hopping into the front seat between us without so much as a squeal.

Gramps turned the key in the ignition and the old sedan came to life. But for a change he didn't gun the engine, probably fearing he'd stir the entire neighbourhood. He threw the gears into reverse, backed carefully down the driveway and paused briefly when the car reached the street. He seemed uncertain which way to head.

"Do you mind telling me where we're going?" I said.

"I'm not sure," Gramps said. His voice was quiet, steady. "All I know is, we're going somewhere. *Any*where."

The car stood in the roadway, the gears in neutral now, the engine idling quietly.

"I don't get it," I said. "It's going on midnight, the three of us are sitting in this car, and you haven't got a *clue* where we're going?"

"I've got to get away, Ben," Gramps said, staring ahead along the dimly lit street. "All my life, it seems I've been climbing a ladder. And now, when I'm darn near at the top, it looks like I leaned it against the wrong wall. None of what I have to do makes sense to me any more."

With that explanation, and nothing more, Grandfather threw the car into first and we took off. All I knew was, we were heading south. I was confused, more than a little scared, and convinced of only one thing, that the man at the wheel was out of his mind.

# Fourteen

**A**ccording to Mabel Walmsley who waited on him at the Kozy Korner that morning, Hollis Burden was the happiest-looking man in the whole of Port Sanford. "Lemme have an order of ham 'n eggs, Mabel," Hollis said, straddling a lunch-counter stool as if it was a saddle. "And gimme a side of fries and a coupla them buttermilk pancakes instead of toast. Coffee, double cream. Oh, yes, orange juice for starters, make it a large."

Mabel had waited on the sheriff's deputy every morning of the week for years. Toast and black coffee was his traditional fare that hour of the day. A tired scowl was his traditional expression. After shouting, "Ham plus two with a side of fries," over her shoulder to the cook, Mabel said, trying to sound casual, not too inquisitive, "You — uh — celebrating something, Hollis?"

Burden smacked his lips. "Yep, sure am."

"Betcha won the lottery last night, huh?"

"Better'n that, Mabel. Much better."

Like everyone else in Port Sanford, Mabel Walmsley knew that in Hollis Burden's line of work occasions to celebrate *any*-thing were few and far between. After all, serving nasty court documents on folks in financial trouble, and carting away their precious belongings to be locked away in some fortress-like warehouse, was nobody's idea of a fun way to earn one's living. The rumour around Port Sanford (I later learned on good authority that Grandfather was responsible for spreading it) was that even Hollis Burden's *mother* despised him. So what could possibly have made the man appear so positively radiant on this particular morning?

"Gotta button my lip for the moment," Hollis said to Mabel, grinning, relishing his new status in Mabel's eyes as a man of mystery. "But it'll all come out soon. And when it does — "

At the time, Mabel Walmsley had no way of knowing the reason for her customer's apparent high spirits. The reason was simple: In his pinched nostrils, Hollis Burden was certain he detected the tantalizing aroma of revenge. Revenge against whom? Why, Ira Lamport of course. Ever since their confrontation years earlier at Hilda's Diner, Burden had chewed on the bitter herb of humiliation, vowing to anybody who would listen that he would even the score with my grandfather even if it meant flying to the moon.

And now — now, at long last — Hollis Burden's archenemy, Ira Lamport, had handed him a golden opportunity to do so.

It happened this way: An anxious telephone call early that morning from Agnes Trimble to the Port Sanford chief of police had started the story of our flight snowballing through town. "I can't imagine where they would've gone but a next-door neighbour said she heard the car start up and leave late last night," Agnes reported to the chief, her voice on the edge of cracking. "All I know is, Mr. Lamport stuck a note in my typewriter saying 'Gone away. Took Ben and Josh. Look after things.'"

"Who's Ben?" the Chief said.

"Mr. Lamport's grandson."

"And Josh?"

"Rebecca O'Hearn's dog … a Chihuahua."

She heard the Chief guffaw. "A chi-*what*?"

"A Chihuahua."

"Th'heck good's a dog like that? Ira'd been better off hiring a hamster for protection. At least they stay awake all night."

Agnes said, beginning to get annoyed, "He didn't take the dog along for protection, I assure you." How dared the Chief make fun of Ira Lamport! "Anyway, I'm worried sick about Mr. Lamport, Chief. He's been acting kind of strange these last few days, especially since Rebecca O'Hearn's funeral."

"Anything unusual around his house?"

"No," Agnes said, "except his housekeeper Mrs. Bjorklund says by the look of their bedrooms it seems they packed their things in a hurry."

Despite the anxiety in her voice, the Chief refused to get excited. "Sounds to me like maybe they just decided on the spur of the moment to take off and go fishing, maybe to one of them fancy camps up around Manitoulin Island where the Americans like to fish. Or something like that. Word around the courthouse lately is that old Ira's overdue for a vacation, y'know."

"Now listen to me, Chief," Agnes Trimble said, her voice rising, "Ira Lamport wouldn't know a fishing rod from a lightning rod. I just feel in my bones that there's something terribly wrong about their disappearance. Can't you issue an all-points bulletin, or whatever it is you people do when somebody's gone missing?"

It was the Chief's turn to become annoyed. "Now hold on a minute, Miss Trimble. There's nothing says this is a case of missing persons. I don't know where on earth you got the idea there's a disappearance going on here."

"You mean you're going to sit there and do nothing about this?"

"Yes," the chief yelled into the telephone, "that's exactly

what I'm going to do until I see or hear some real evidence that there's maybe some foul play. I can't take time to deal with every crank call — "

"*Crank call!*" Agnes, recalling that conversation later, admitted to me that she'd never slammed a telephone in anybody's ear in her life until that moment.

The next moment she was on the telephone to the Sheriff's office. A man's voice answered. "Sorry, ma'am, the Sheriff's in Ottawa at a convention. Can I help you?"

Agnes Trimble repeated the fears she had expressed minutes before in her call to the chief of police. The man at the other end of the line sounded keenly interested. "I'll look into this personally, ma'am," he assured Miss Trimble. "Believe me, I share your concern."

The man at the other end of the line was Hollis Burden.

If Ira Lamport had mysteriously fled Port Sanford last night, it could only mean one thing: The old coot must have absconded with Rebecca O'Hearn's money. After all, didn't it make perfect sense? A batty old woman with pots of gold stashed away in some locked-up cave ... a wily old lawyer trusted with the keys ...

The trick was to go after Ira right away, while his tracks were fresh. Don't give him a chance to get too far away. If he had the kid and the dog towing behind him, that would slow him down for sure.

Burden swung into action.

Within minutes of Agnes Trimble's call, he organized a meeting at his office with the Medleys and their sister Priscilla. When his visitors (now his clients) started to take their leave, the receptionist in the outer office overheard Priscilla wish Hollis Godspeed, heard Hollis assure them he would not fail in his mission, saw the Sheriff's deputy rub his hands together and grin with satisfaction after they'd gone.

# Fifteen

**B**urden no doubt pictured himself launching a heroic one-man crusade to seek us out, capture us — especially to capture my grandfather — and bring us back alive. Hollis Burden, stalwart officer of the law, marching the three of us (yes, Josh included) single-handedly down Port Sanford's main street ... what a sight, what a triumph! At last the town's citizens, those same gullible fools who for decades had regarded Ira Lamport as a pillar of the community, a champion of the underdog, would come to realize what a scoundrel, what a shameless faker, the old lawyer truly was. There would be front-page pictures and headlines, a civic reception hosted by the mayor, letters of praise from the bishop of the diocese and the premier of the province, maybe even a medal (well, why not?) from the attorney general for service beyond the call of duty.

Let the hunt begin!

Confident that at the moment he, and he alone, was aware of what we were up to, Hollis Burden pulled up at the service station at the edge of town where the Sheriff's officers routinely gassed up.

"'Mornin', Hollis," said Ted Burns, getting ready to thrust the pump into the side of the Jeep. "Usual five dollars?"

"Nope," said Burden, "Better fill 'er up."

"Fill 'er up? You must be headin' to South America, huh?"

"None of your business," was all Hollis Burden said.

Where the Port Sanford cut-off hits Highway 35, just before the traffic lights, Hollis Burden pulled over to the gravel shoulder and came to a stop. Born and raised in this area, he knew the countryside from one end to the other. Every side road and single-lane right-of-way was as familiar to him as the lines and wrinkles of his own face. In the course of tracking down people hiding themselves or their property from the forces of the law, Burden had driven his Jeep, and several Jeeps before the current one, through all manner of unfriendly terrain — back roads barely wide enough for a horse and cart, even through rough bush country where deer and moose travelled with difficulty. He told himself those would not be the highways and byways of a man like Ira Lamport.

What was it Lamport was always telling people? Yes, of course! He hated big cities. Didn't just dislike them or despise them. *Hated* them. Especially the worst big city of all: Toronto. There was hardly a soul in Port Sanford who hadn't heard the old lawyer's outspoken contempt for the capital city of the province. "Everybody's out to get their hand in your pocket," Lamport would say of Toronto, "and it doesn't matter what they do for a living — politicians, thieves, stockbrokers, panhandlers, even the guy that runs a hot dog stand — you close your eyes for two seconds and you're lucky you've still got your underwear."

"Well, Ira," people would say, prodding him gently, "how come your own flesh and blood chooses to live there if it's so gawdawful?"

"My daughter," Grandfather would shoot back, "suffers from the deadliest form of exposure that can beset a young woman — a liberal education."

Burden's eyes drifted first to the landscape on his right, following Highway 35's remarkably straight-as-an-arrow course northward.

Now Hollis Burden shifted his gaze to his left, to where the highway stretched, again with remarkable directness, southward, southward to the Forbidden City — Toronto.

And then, in a flash, the answer came to Hollis Burden.

Toronto was the last place on this earth that one would expect to find Ira Lamport.

Therefore, much as he professed to loathe the very name "Toronto," Toronto is precisely where Ira Lamport — that cunning old fox — would head for. Ah, but not *downtown* Toronto, because that's where all the big fancy hotels were located and everyone knew that Ira Lamport wasn't a man to part with his dollars for luxury accommodations. Besides, checking into a major downtown hotel with a thirteen-year-old boy and a dog (even if the dog was acceptable) would attract too much attention.

No, Ira would most likely hole up in some cheap suburban motel, maybe even use an assumed name, convince the kid to go along with the alias. As for the dog, well, it would be pretty tough to train an old Chihuahua to respond to a new name, but Hollis wouldn't put it past Gramps to try.

To Toronto, then, Burden must have told himself, no doubt smiling slyly, thinking that it took a fox to outfox a fox.

# Sixteen

L ife is one imperfect thing after another, and in Hollis
Burden's case there was something he hadn't counted on
— Mrs. Bjorklund, Grandfather's housekeeper.

When it came to spreading the news of the day, Mrs.
Bjorklund was far more timely and effective than the once-a-
week *Port Sanford Echo*. This woman, who seldom spoke
unless she was spoken to while on duty, after hours became
a fountain of information, gushing facts, rumours, speculations,
revelations, confidences and hunches in all directions. So it was
that, by the time Hollis Burden's earnest little black Jeep
(Gramps called it the Black Jeep of The Burden Family) had
covered the first few miles on his southward quest, dozens of
citizens had already heard the fast-breaking news, and dozens
more were about to hear it.

"Imagine," she must have said. "It's the middle of the night
and for some terrible reason off the three of them go ... yes,
the dog too! ... disappeared into the darkness, they did, the
old man distraught over some horrible mistake he'd made concerning Mrs. O'Hearn's will ... He'd had a serious falling-out
with her next-of-kin ... He'd made off with all the trust funds
in her estate in all likelihood ... The whole affair was a disaster (his own secretary had used that word, "disaster")...The

three of them were probably heading for some remote part of the United States where nobody would ever dream of finding them ... That mouthy grandson of Ira's was probably dragged into this sordid business for no purpose other than to keep an eye on that obnoxious little animal that was nothing more than six pounds of noise and fleas."

As they were bound to do, these unhappy tidings soon reached the ears of Port Sanford's Chief of Police, Harley Davidson, the same police chief who, earlier that morning, had dismissed Agnes Trimble's anxiety as though she were telephoning to report a missing canary.

Two facts concerning the Chief distinguished him among his colleagues in the profession of law enforcement. First, his father, Tom Davidson, had been Port Sanford's police chief a generation earlier. Having begun his career as a motorcycle patrolman, the senior Davidson figured that the highest honour he could bestow upon his only begotten son was to name the boy Harley. When the son took up a career in police work, it turned out that the young officer possessed the durability of the motorcycles after which he was named, but not the swiftness. This led to the second fact: Chief Harley Davidson's unblemished record for taking action in cases of suspected crime only after the volcano had erupted and the lava was setting fire to his boots.

Reaching Agnes Trimble, who by now was poring through files and papers on my grandfather's desk in a frantic search for clues as to our whereabouts, Chief Davidson apologized for his initial indifference. "Look, Miss Trimble, summer's a busy time for us, lots of traffic accidents on the roads, weekend drinking bouts, family fights, that sorta stuff. We got our priorities, you understand. That's how come I didn't take your call as seriously as I should've."

Stiffly, Agnes said, "I accept your apology, Chief, but I

already have somebody attending to the case, thank you very much."

"Oh? Mind telling me who?"

"Yes," said Agnes, "a very nice, sensitive man at the Sheriff's Office. *He*, I'm happy to say, took my call seriously."

"Couldn't've been Sheriff Ambrose. He's at a convention in Ottawa. You got any idea who you spoke to, Miss Trimble?"

"No, I don't. I was so upset at the time I didn't bother to get his name. Anyway, what's it matter? The point is, *some-body's* on the job at the Sheriff's Office, which is more than one can say about the Police Department."

Chief Davidson accepted this rebuke without argument. Politely, he said, "My department'll do everything we can to find Mr. Lamport, see to it that he's returned safe and sound. The kid and the dog, too."

The Chief's next call was to the Sheriff's Office. "It's Chief Davidson," he barked over the phone. "Gimme Hollis Burden."

"I'm sorry," said the Sheriff's receptionist, "Mr. Burden checked out early this morning. I'm not expecting him back today."

"He say where he was going?"

"No. Just that he had a tough assignment out of town."

Next the Chief was on the line to Ted Burns at the gas station. "Teddy, you seen Hollis Burden at all today?"

"Yeah," Burns said, "Hollis was in a while ago. Did something he doesn't always do, even though it's government money."

"Meaning what?"

"Meaning he went for a full tank of gas instead of the usual five bucks' worth."

"Hollis say where he was headed?"

"Nope, but I got the impression it was someplace pretty far off. Besides, you know Hollis, Chief. Gets that bloodhound look on his face, like he's got wind of somebody's scent. Ain't nothing gonna stop him, know what I mean?"

No additional explanation was necessary. A full tank of gas in Hollis Burden's Jeep meant one thing only: Hollis Burden must be in pursuit of his long-time foe, Ira Lamport. And if Lamport was as guilty as rumours suggested, chances were the old lawyer was trying to put as much distance as possible between himself and Port Sanford.

Davidson was bothered by one question: If the Medley brothers and their sister Priscilla were so certain that they were being defrauded by the lawyer for their aunt's estate, why didn't they come to *him*? After all, he, Harley Davidson, was the supreme law enforcer in this region. Apprehending Ira Lamport was a job for the Port Sanford Police Department, not some two-bit bill collector in a beat-up Jeep.

But then Davidson began doing some figuring. He looked at it this way: If *police* were to catch up with Ira Lamport, they'd be obliged to arrest him and lay charges. There would be criminal investigations. A trial. A conviction. A jail term. The old man would lose his licence to practise law. Lose his property. End up penniless. That way the Medleys and their sister Priscilla might not see one red cent of the O'Hearn estate money.

On the other hand, with Hollis giving chase, once Gramps was tracked down and cornered, there might be a chance to salvage most of the O'Hearn fortune without all the police rigmarole. Besides, it was a safe bet that the old lady's heirs had promised Burden that a speedy capture of Ira Lamport before all the money vanished would earn the deputy a lot more than a reward in heaven.

Still, the thought of Hollis Burden pursuing Gramps did not sit well with Chief Harley Davidson. "It's up to *me* to go after old Ira," he said to himself.

But where to find Gramps?

Simple. Find Hollis Burden.

Bounding from his private office, he called out to two uniformed constables who were about to leave the police station for mid-day patrol, "Carter, Thompson ... hold everything!"

The two policemen stopped in their tracks. Carter, the elder of the two, said, "What's up, boss?"

"I want you two to head north on Highway 35. Find out if Hollis Burden's been seen driving up that way in his Jeep. I'm heading south on 35 in case he's on his way down to Toronto. Keep me posted, y'hear?"

"Hollis in some kinda trouble?" Officer Thompson asked.

"I got no time to explain right now. All I'm saying is, if you manage to get on his trail, follow him *but under no circumstances are you to stop him*. Is that clear? Just keep your eyes on him, find out his destination and then report back to me. If *I* manage to track him down, I'll let you know and you can scrub the rest of the mission. Now better get a move on, there's no time to lose."

# Seventeen

T hinking back to that crazy night and the twenty-four hours that followed, I'm forced to admit one important fact about Hollis Burden: The man was shrewd. He was petty, officious, vindictive, unlovable, spiteful, cheap, underhanded ... yes, all these things and more. But he was also shrewd. Shrewd because he managed to add two and two and come up with five for an answer. Put another way, Hollis' guess about our destination was a hundred and ten percent correct.

"So we're heading for Toronto after all," I said, sounding surprised. I figured if Gramps was anxious to disappear for a while, he would have chosen to go north. "As long as we're going down to the city, you might as well drop me off at my dad's apartment, if you don't mind." I said. "I can bunk in with him until Mom returns from Europe."

Grandfather took his eyes off the road long enough to give me a look that suggested I was insane. "Not a chance!" he snapped. "The last thing I need right now is an encounter with your father. Stick with me, there'll never be a dull moment."

At this point, a dull moment seemed very appealing to me. I was sure that before long we would be on a nationwide "Most Wanted" list. "Everybody's going to be after us," I said. "I bet the Mounties and FBI are on the lookout for us already."

"Ridiculous!" Grandfather pointed to the clock on the dashboard. It was not yet midnight. "We haven't even been on the road a half-hour yet," he said. "Nobody's going to know we've gone until tomorrow morning when Agnes finds the note I've left for her stuck in her typewriter. By that time we'll be set up somewhere in Toronto where they can't find us. We'll be like three needles in a haystack. I've never made a secret of the fact that I hate Toronto, so nobody'd *dream* of finding me there. It'll give me some time to collect my thoughts, develop a proper sense of direction."

"Well, that's just great," I said, making no effort to conceal my sarcasm. "And while you're collecting your thoughts and developing your proper sense of direction, what'm *I* supposed to be doing?"

"One: You will be in charge of Josh. Two: You're to maintain a constant lookout, making sure we're not being followed. Remember: Eternal vigilance is the price of freedom."

"Where are we going to stay?"

"You'll know when we get there."

"*How* will I know?"

"Because the car will have come to a full stop and the engine will be turned off. Now do me a favour, Ben. Call off the interrogation and let me concentrate on the driving. Get some sleep if you want to."

"I thought part of my job is to maintain eternal vigilance. Now you're telling me to get some sleep?" I shook my head. "There are times, Gramps, when I really don't understand you."

"That's okay, Ben," Grandfather said quietly. "There are times when I really don't understand my*self*."

Hours later, I felt my arm being shaken. "Ben, wake up — "

My eyes felt as though someone had poured sand into them. When I rubbed them open, the first thing I saw was a neon sign, its bright red glow assaulting me, forcing me to blink until

I became accustomed to it. The sign simply read "PLEAS-ANTVIEW MOTEL — VACANCY."

The car had come to a full stop and the engine was turned off, which meant we'd arrived. Arrived where? Somewhere, that was all I knew.

"This looks as good a place as any," Grandfather said. "Wait here while I see if we can check in."

"Where are we?"

"Outskirts of Toronto."

"What time is it?"

"Little after four."

My eyes refused to stay open. "You mean a.m. or p.m.?" I asked.

"See for yourself," Gramps said, getting out of the car.

I heard the crunch of his shoes on the gravel driveway as he made his way to the motel office, the only part of the place that had lights burning at this hour. A few cars were parked here and there, in front of the occupied units. I could hear the sounds of buses and trucks rumbling by. From a field behind the motel came the sound of crickets, their steady rhythm like the ticking of a clock drifting over the landscape in the cool night air.

I was feeling chilled and miserable but before I could wallow in self-pity Grandfather was back at the car.

"Come, Ben, and bring the dog. We've got a room for the night. We'll lock the car and leave it right here. Our unit's just ahead, Number Three."

In the darkness I couldn't tell whether or not the Pleasantview Motel lived up to its name. Were there lakes nearby? Green hillsides? A stand of shade trees? A lush valley off in the distance? Farmers' gardens where the crickets sunned themselves or kept cool in the shade between the stalks of corn?

I would have to wait until morning to find out. But as Gramps unlocked the door to Unit Three, switched on a single overhead light and we entered, something told me the view outdoors would be as bleak as the sight indoors. The two narrow beds were covered in bedspreads that might have been white a long time ago but now were the colour of porridge. Between the beds stood a rickety night table that looked as if it had been painted brown over and over again until the wood had disappeared and only the coats of paint were keeping it standing. A smudged mirror over the small chest of drawers reflected the ugliness of the room.

"Where's the TV, Gramps?" I asked, knowing in my heart there was none.

"What do you expect for nine dollars a night, Buckingham Palace?" Gramps replied. He had flopped himself down on one of the beds after removing only his jacket and shoes, and without bothering to remove the bedspread. "Turn off the light, will you, Ben — "

I wanted to ask how long he intended to keep the three of us imprisoned here but before I could utter another word I saw that he was sound asleep, snoring softly, his long legs stretched out like stilts, his mouth and jaw exhibiting the kind of slackness that goes with exhaustion.

# Eighteen

**D**id I say Hollis Burden was shrewd? Perhaps there's a better adjective to describe him: persistent. Hollis' occupation as Deputy Sheriff in charge of searches and seizures didn't call for a great and noble mind. What the job required was a man whose nose was seldom more than an inch or two from the ground, a man who, once he caught even the faintest whiff of his target, could toss aside everything — food, rest, the ordinary comforts of life, family, friends (what few there were). Hollis Burden, born hunter, skilful at guessing his quarry's next moves. I can see him in action as if I'd been sitting beside him in his Jeep.

Along the route Hollis Burden keeps his eyes on motels and roadside restaurants. He stops at one or another to inquire if the proprietors have seen us. None has.

Reasoning — again correctly — that Gramps would have tired himself out after three or four hours of late night driving, Hollis concludes that in all likelihood we have sought shelter at the first cheap-looking dump on our route.

The first cheap-looking dump turns out to be the Pleasantview Motel. Burden glances at his watch. It is now going on five o'clock in the afternoon. He pulls into the gravel driveway, gets out of the Jeep and, shielding his eyes from the sun beating down on that treeless plot of land, surveys the parking spaces. No sign of my grandfather's old Buick. Talk to the boss inside anyway. Maybe, just maybe, Hollis thinks.

"Hi, there," Hollis says, tipping his hat, hoping a show of politeness will charm the woman behind the reception desk. The motel office smells of stale coffee. "That coffee sure smells good. Hope I'm not interrupting your supper, ma'am," says Hollis, oozing amiability.

"You looking for a room for the night?" the woman says, reaching for the registration book.

"Not exactly," Hollis says. "What I'm really looking for is an elderly gent, kinda tall, bit stooped. Travelling with a kid about thirteen. Oh, yes, and a dog. Thought they might've checked in here late last night or early this morning."

The woman frowns. "A dog, you say? They wouldn't have got a room here with a dog. We don't allow pets, 'specially dogs."

"Well, you gotta understand, ma'am, the dog in question is just a teeny bit of a thing. One of them Chihuahuas, y'know, like so big— " Using his hands Hollis indicates the height and length of a Chihuahua. "A person could almost stick one of 'em in his shirt pocket and you'd never notice."

"We got a firm rule against pets," the woman says grimly.

"I'm sure you do, ma'am." Hollis casts a quick glance outside. "Looks to me like you run a really first-rate establishment. Real convenient, too, having a meat-packing plant just across the road, next to that auto wrecking yard."

"So you don't need a room?" The woman starts to close the registration book.

"No, ma'am. Like I said, I need to find the man I described to you. Mind if I look at your register?"

"You some kind of police officer?" the woman aks, her hand firmly on the closed book.

"Well, not exactly."

"We don't go showing who's registered here to any Tom, Dick and Harry comes in off the street."

Hollis flashes the woman the broadest smile he can manufacture. "And so you shouldn't. By all means, a person in charge of a fine establishment like yours has to be mighty careful. But maybe you can just tell me if a man about seventy-five and his grandson are checked into one of your units, the old one driving a Buick that's seen better days. I'd sure be grateful for your help."

"They in some kinda trouble?"

"No, not at all, ma'am. Matter of fact, I'm a Sheriff's officer, Hollis Burden, from Port Sanford just up 35, y'know. And I'm trying to locate them to tell them some good news."

"Like what?"

Hollis thinks fast. "Well, you see, every summer, this time of July, Port Sanford's Chamber of Commerce runs a draw. First prize is really something! A new car, a trailer and motorboat, and a thousand dollars."

"You saying the old man won all that?"

"That's what I'm saying. Trouble is, he'd left town and the head of the Chamber of Commerce has sent me to fetch him back. There's to be a big award ceremony at the Town Hall tomorrow."

"Lucky fella," says the woman, shaking her head. "Me, I gotta sit in this office day after day, night after night, year after year. Never won a thing in my life."

"I know how you feel, ma'am," Hollis says, nodding sympathetically. "I'm just a workin' stiff myself."

"They're checked into Unit Three," the woman says.

"Thank you, thank you very, very much, ma'am." Quickly Hollis turns to leave.

"You won't find them in, though," the woman adds. "I heard

'em say something about going for supper. But I sure didn't see any trace of a dog. They left here about half an hour ago, I'd say."

"Did you happen to hear where they were going for supper?" Hollis asks.

"No. Lots of folks that stay here end up at a little hamburger joint, Barney's, a mile or so down the road. Or they might've gone to Primrose Fish and Chips a little farther along. Or maybe Chicken King, about another mile south. On the other hand, they could've — "

Hollis Burden doesn't wait for the woman to finish rambling on about the variety of eating places in the area. Shouting, "Thanks again," over his shoulder, he makes a dash for the Jeep and takes off.

As luck had it, while Hollis was setting new speed records in search of us, Gramps and I had finished hamburgers at Barney's and headed back to the Pleasantview Motel. Entering the office to pick up the key for Unit Three, Gramps was greeted by the owner. "Say there," she called out cheerfully, "there's been a man here, some sheriff's officer from Port Sanford up north, looking for you. Says you won a lottery or something and they want you back up there to pick up your prizes. A car, boat and cash. By the way, sir, you got a dog, by any chance?"

Gramps ignored the question. "The man give his name?"

"Hollis something."

"Hollis Burden?"

"Yeah. Hollis Burden."

Grandfather pretended to be pleased. "Well, now, that's mighty good news. We'll be checking out now, ma'am."

The woman looked astonished. "Right this minute, you mean?"

"Absolutely. What do I owe you?"

We were packed and out of Unit Three ten minutes later,

Grandfather pushing the Buick to the limit of its capacity as we entered the city, threading our way through thickening traffic.

Returning to the Pleasantview Motel, Hollis Burden barges into the office. His forehead glistens with sweat and his sparse black hair is matted. Scowling, he shouts to the woman behind the reception desk, "They musta come back here. They weren't at any of the places you told me. Which way to Unit Three?"

"Oh, you're too late," the woman says. "They left a while ago. I'd say at least a half-hour. I told them you were looking for them, about winning the prize and all. The old gentleman said they were going right back to Port Sanford, like you wanted. By the way, sir, you sure they had a dog with them?"

"Never mind," Burden grumbles.

"Would you be wanting a room for the night, then? Unit Three's available."

"Aw, shut up," Hollis Burden says, stalking out of the office, slamming the door behind him.

Then he pulls out of the driveway and swings southward, in the direction of the city he knows Ira Lamport hates with a passion.

About an hour after Hollis Burden's hasty departure, a black car with white markings and a red light on its roof pulled into the gravel driveway in front of the Pleasantview Motel. Its single uniformed occupant climbed out, stretched his bulky figure and then strode into the office.

"Yes, officer, what can I do for you?" the proprietor said.

"I'm Chief Harley Davidson, Port Sanford Police Department," the man said. "Wonder if maybe you can help me. I'm looking for a man by the name of Hollis Burden — "

# Nineteen

At the first exit sign pointing in the direction of downtown Toronto, Gramps made a sudden left turn, giving rise to an angry chorus of horns from motorists behind us. Starting down one of the wide main arteries that fed into the heart of the city, we found ourselves engulfed in heavy traffic even though it was past the evening rush hour. "My God," Grandfather grumbled, "don't these people have homes? They must spend their pitiful existence inhaling their own exhaust fumes!"

He was leaning stiffly over the steering wheel, the bony fingers of one hand gripping the rim like a horse's reins, the other hand hovering over the horn ready to blast to kingdom come anyone or anything that dared to approach within shouting distance. His right foot flip-flopped constantly from gas pedal to brake and back with the regularity of a windshield wiper. At red lights the old Buick lurched to a stop, then lurched forward again like a bucking bronco when the lights turned green. Whenever a light was amber Grandfather's foot fluttered uncertainly over the pedals. Should he stop? Go? Or simply throw up his hands and let the car decide?

At last I spoke up. "Is it true," I asked, "that when you get to be seventy-five the government makes you take a test before they renew your driver's licence?"

"Where'd you hear a dumb thing like that?"

"Dad told me the day I was getting ready to take the bus up to Port Sanford. I asked how come he couldn't drive me up and he said he was up to his eyeballs with work. So I asked why *you* couldn't drive down to Toronto to pick me up."

"And he said? — "

"He said he'd driven with you once a couple of years ago and that — uh — well, it really doesn't matter now, I guess."

"Well, go ahead, tell me. After all, you've never exactly been the soul of discretion."

"Soul of discretion? — "

"Knowing when to speak and when *not* to speak."

"Uh-huh. Well, in that case, I remember he used the word 'menace.' Something about drivers your age being a menace on the roads."

Grandfather snorted. "If Talbot Marshall had his way people my age would be set adrift on ice floes and left to freeze to death. God help your father when he gets to be an old man and can't handle a scalpel any longer."

"All the same," I said, "I think we should call him now that we're in the city. After all, he *is* my dad, so he should know what's happening, where I am, where we're going ... or *not* going."

Grandfather pointed to the lines of bumper-to-bumper traffic on all sides. "Let me get us out of this mess first," he said, "then I'll think about contacting my dear ex-son-in-law. Meantime, Ben, you keep your eyes peeled. You see any sign of a black Jeep with a guy at the wheel looks like a coyote, you yell. You yell good and loud."

"But you told the woman back at the motel we were heading right back to Port Sanford."

"What I told *her* doesn't matter a darn. What matters is what Hollis Burden believes and he's nobody's fool. I'll bet my last dollar he's not far behind us right this minute. It'd be nothing short of a miracle if he went in the opposite direction."

"Maybe we should be praying for a miracle," I said.

I wanted all this to come to an end, to be over and done with as quickly as possible. If Gramps had fled Port Sanford because he'd done something seriously wrong, let them catch up to him, take him back and get him to face the music. Enough of this craziness.

"You keeping an eye out behind us?" Grandfather asked, checking up on me as we approached a busy intersection and came to a halt.

"Sure," I said, twisting about in my seat and looking out the rear window. "Nothing but a long line of regular cars," I reported. "No sign of a black Jeep."

That was a lie.

Not more than four or five cars behind us, I spotted a black Jeep nosing out of line. In a flash it became plain that the driver was desperately attempting to get ahead of the pack and draw up as close as possible to my grandfather's car. Perhaps he might even head us off by the time we crossed the intersection.

"All clear so far, Ben?"

"All clear," I answered, doubling the lie.

The traffic light turned green. Grandfather's foot shot to the accelerator. The old Buick coughed, then leapt forward. As it did, I looked past my grandfather. In the lane to our left I caught sight of the front end of the Jeep. A second or two later the driver came into view. His eyes were focused on us, one hand motioning us wildly to pull over. He seemed to be paying not the slightest attention to traffic behind or in front of him. He was determined not to let us out of sight even for the blink of an eye.

And then Grandfather spotted him. "What the — !" he shouted, jamming his foot down hard on the accelerator and pulling well ahead of Burden. "That's *him*, all right. That's Hollis!" Without looking at me, he said, "You told me there was no sign of him. You lost your eyesight, boy, or what?"

"I'm sorry," I said. "I guess with all this traffic — "

"You *guess*!" Grandfather said, his expression and voice full of scorn. "I was *depending* on you, Ben. Now look what's happening."

Nervously, I asked, "What're we going to do?"

"*We*?" Grandfather said. "You mean what am *I* going to do. You're certainly no help at all. Here's what *I'm* going to do. You just watch me."

# Twenty

My grandfather's Buick wove in and out of traffic like a skier in a slalom race. We changed lanes. We made sudden stops. We made even more sudden starts. We made abrupt turns, sometimes left in the face of oncoming cars, sometimes right, cutting off cars behind us. Yellow lights? No longer a matter of uncertainty. Gramps simply barrelled through the intersection, scarcely paying attention to traffic crossing his path.

Hunched over the wheel, his fingers welded solidly to the rim, Grandfather was determined to accomplish two goals: first, to shake loose once and for all from Hollis Burden, and second, to prove how wrong my father was about his driving skill.

I could do nothing but sit on the passenger side frozen to the seat, shutting my eyes tightly at times to avoid witnessing what I was convinced would be a disastrous ending for the three of us.

Josh, too, seemed frozen, as though his canine brain could sense the risks to which we were being exposed. Perched on my lap, he enjoyed one important advantage over me: because of his small size he could not see over the dashboard and was therefore spared the actual sight of Grandfather's terrifying manoeuvres through the busy streets.

After Gramps had ignored three stop signs in a row, oblivious to all the screeching brakes and honking horns surrounding him, I finally piped up, "You just went clean through another intersection without coming to a full stop!"

" 'Full stop' is a phrase that's capable of many definitions," he shot back. "Fact is, I took the trouble to look both ways before proceeding. Far as I'm concerned, that amounts to a full stop."

"Is that the law, or did you just make it up?"

"It's called creative thinking," Grandfather said. "Some day, if you're ever smart enough to be a lawyer, you'll learn that what's written in the law books is *one* thing; what's written *between* the lines is another. Now shut up, Ben, and let me drive."

"But can't we at least slow down a little?" I pleaded. Looking quickly over my shoulder, I added, "Honest, Gramps, that black Jeep is nowhere in sight. I swear."

I found myself praying that a police cruiser would spy us and bring this mad ride to a halt. But if there was a police force in Toronto, they must all have gone into hiding. There was not a single patrol car in sight for blocks.

My grandfather maintained what could generally be described as a southbound course. Before long, I caught sight for the first time of the waterfront. If he stayed on this course, within minutes we would find ourselves momentarily floating on and rapidly sinking into Lake Ontario.

"Gramps," I began hesitantly, "I hate to interrupt you at a time like this — "

"Then don't," Grandfather snapped, speeding up.

"But we're heading straight for the lake and this car hasn't got wings."

"Don't need wings. I can fly without 'em."

As he said this, Grandfather executed another of his spectacular unexpected right turns. We were speeding west now along Lakeshore Boulevard, approaching the Canadian National Exhibition grounds. Hundreds of cars were around us, all of them pouring into the grounds.

"Any sign of Hollis now?" Grandfather asked.

I looked behind us. "None."

"You absolutely sure, or just guessing?"

"I'm absolutely, positively sure."

"You were sure once before, back there when we hit the city. You telling me the truth now?"

Obviously my grandfather's confidence in me was far from restored. "Are you calling me a liar?" I said.

"I'm not calling you anything," he replied. "Just don't let me down again, boy. Loyalty, that's what's expected. Now hang on — "

With one swift motion, my grandfather swung the car out of our lane and into one that was moving more quickly into the exhibition grounds. Another swift motion and we were in the vast parking lot. A third and the Buick came to a sputtering, coughing rest in a space where it would not stand out, a space surrounded by hundreds of parked cars.

"Come," Grandfather commanded. "And bring Josh. No sense leaving the poor dog alone."

"Where are we going?" I asked, holding Josh in my arms as I got out of the car.

"We're going to the fair, kiddies," Grandfather said with exaggerated cheerfulness.

"Fair? What fair?"

"Read the signs, boy."

I peered at a sign near the parking lot entrance. It read,

"Welcome To The Annual Canadian National Summer Fair."

There was a satisfied smile on my grandfather's face. "That sharp-eyed coyote'd never *dream* of finding us here," he said, as though talking to himself.

# Twenty-one

"Take a whiff of that air, Ben! There's nothing like it, nothing!"

We were in the cavernous main exhibition hall now. My grandfather had stopped in his tracks, oblivious to the crowds surging past him. There was a look of contentment on his face that I'd never seen before. His eyes were closed and he was inhaling deeply. I felt no urge to breathe that deeply. My nostrils were already rejecting the pungent aromas of farm animals wafting all the way from the stables and pens at the far end of the building. Sniffing and grimacing, I said, "I guess that smell's okay if you don't care what gets into your lungs."

Grandfather took this as a personal insult. "That's your own family background you're slandering, boy," he said. Eyeing me with a contemptuous look, he said, "I suppose to a city kid like you carbon monoxide fumes are preferable."

"If it's all the same to you," I said, "I'd rather inhale what comes out of the rear of a *car*."

He gave me a sad look as though he'd just written me off as a human being.

We made our way, or were pushed by the crowd, past row upon row of giant wooden bins filled to their rims with grains of wheat, oats, corn and barley, each bin tagged with the grower's name. Then came tables laden with preserves — jams, pickles, relishes, whole vegetables — labelled with names like Elizabeth Handley, Myrtle Crispin and Sue-Ellen McCandless, names that conjured up in my mind grey-haired ladies in aprons and sleeveless flowered dresses, with pudgy pink arms, standing over hot stoves stirring huge steaming vats of berries and cucumbers and spices. For years I had steadfastly turned down invitations to visit the summer fair. Now I knew for certain why. It all looked so endless, so terribly down-to-earth, so boring.

"How long are we going to be stuck hiding out here?" I asked Grandfather. He didn't bother to respond. Instead, his face lit up. His eyes had landed on a manufacturer's display of shiny farm implements. "My God," Gramps exclaimed, "look at that tractor, Ben. Isn't it a beauty? What I would've given when I was your age to have a tractor like that!"

I was having difficulty sharing Grandfather's excitement. "Did your dad allow you to borrow the family tractor whenever you had a date?" I said.

Grandfather looked at me sternly. "I suppose you think that's funny?"

"I'm sorry you're not amused," I said, "but the truth is, a tractor is just a horse with four wheels."

He stood glaring at me, his hands on his hips, a sign always that his patience was running out. "Is there *any*thing that would possibly interest you here? Or at the tender age of thirteen have you been everywhere and seen everything there is to see?"

I glanced hastily about the hall. "*There*," I said, "there's something I wouldn't mind seeing." I was pointing to an overhead banner that read: "National Dog Show Tonight, 8 p.m., Centre Arena."

"Who needs to see a dog show?" Grandfather said. Looking down at Josh (whom I was obliged to carry since he hadn't come to us supplied with a leash) my grandfather added, "Anyway, we've got a dog show of our own. One dog in my life is more than enough right now."

"Aw, c'mon," I urged, "let's just watch a few minutes of it. I bet it'll be fun. Anyway, that Burden fellow must've given up by now and gone back to Port Sanford."

Grandfather looked at his watch. "Don't be too sure of that. Besides, we still have to find a place to put our heads down for the night."

"It's early. We've got plenty of time to look for a hotel or something," I said.

Looking unhappy, Grandfather said, "Well, all right. But we're not staying long, understand? Half-hour tops. That clear?"

"Perfectly."

The grandstand in the arena was filling up rapidly. My grandfather managed to find a single seat in the first row. Still holding Josh securely in my arms, I squatted at Grandfather's feet, the toes of my shoes just touching the outer edge of the show area. "You lucky dog," I said to Josh. "You've got your-self a ringside seat and you didn't even have to buy a ticket."

Over the loudspeaker system, a deep male voice suddenly boomed, "Good evening, ladies and gentlemen, and welcome to Canada's foremost annual dog show. We will begin this evening's program with the obstacle course competition. But first, let me introduce to you dog lovers our distinguished judge for tonight — "

An overhead spotlight swung across the arena and bathed in its blinding glare a white-haired woman emerging at that moment from a gate and walking with dignified steps to the centre of the ring.

"Please welcome Mrs. Elizabeth Bromley Forsythe, owner of the world-renowned Forsythe Kennels of Greenville, South

Carolina, home to the winners of seven best-of-show trophies at the prestigious annual New York Dog Show — "

Mrs. Forsythe, standing alone now in the middle of the arena, the spotlight still on her, reminded me of a solitary redwood tree. She was tall, stately, very erect and wore a long dark formal gown that made her body look as if it had grown straight up out of the ground.

After acknowledging the audience's applause with a slight bow, Mrs. Forsythe toured the obstacle course. With brisk, firm strides, her expert eyes checked the placement of the ladder and slide, the tunnels constructed from large corrugated steel piping, a zigzag formed by two dozen closely planted wooden staves and a series of fences of varying heights near the end of the course. These the contestants would have to hurdle, making certain to clear the upper bars with all four paws.

Satisfied that the course was laid out according to contest regulations, the judge nodded in the direction of the invisible announcer and returned to the centre of the ring. Again the man's voice boomed out over the loudspeakers. "Judge Forsythe has indicated that the course is in order, ladies and gentlemen, and we're ready to begin. Contestant Number One is 'Troy,' a three-year-old Airedale terrier from the Dumont Kennels of Quebec City, making his debut in this event. Kindly hold your applause until Troy reaches the end of the course, so as not to upset his concentration."

Troy emerged from the starting gate where his owner unleashed him.

It turned out that it wasn't at all difficult to hold our applause; there was very little to applaud. Troy's debut was a disaster. Halfway through the course, the poor dog seemed to sense that he'd made a botch of it, so much so in fact that any attempt to complete the performance would be futile. Dogs have a way of looking sheepish when they blunder (I wonder if sheep have a way of looking doggish when *they* blunder?) and, head down, tail limp, Troy shuffled out of the ring and into the waiting arms of his remarkably forgiving master.

Contestant Number Two looked magnificent and full of confidence. Now there's *my* kind of dog, I thought — a Collie with a nose long and pointed like a sundial, a flowing black, brown and white coat, a graceful tail swinging energetically — definitely my kind of dog.

Alas, as so often happens, looks were deceiving. At the first tunnel, the Collie balked. He too failed to finish and departed the ring in disgrace.

The third contestant, a Boxer named "Fury," fared better, managing to run the entire course in a respectable if not exciting manner. But, like all dogs of her breed, she had a natural scowl on her face that generous applause from the audience failed to soften. No, I thought, a Boxer's not for me.

Number Four, an apricot-coloured Standard Poodle called "Claudette," acquitted herself nicely until she became confused at the zigzag and ran on the outside of it instead of through it, disqualifying herself.

Number Five, "Linus," a brown and white Beagle, was out of sorts from the very beginning and, after mounting the ladder, refused to come down the slide, causing the judge, Mrs. Forsythe — a woman of immense understanding and compassion — to lift him gently from the top of the ladder and return him to his trainer, a distraught teenage girl.

When Number Six, "Chelsea," a Golden Retriever, finished in grand style, I looked down at Josh.

"Take a lesson, Josh," I said. "*That's* how it's done, boy!"

My grip on Josh must have been loose at that moment, for no sooner had I uttered these words than the Chihuahua, without so much as a bark, leapt from my arms. Before I could spring to my feet to retrieve him he was well on his way to the starting point of the obstacle course. I heard Grandfather's voice shouting behind me. "My God, Ben, what've you done? He's got away ... my God!"

I started out toward the far end of the ring, where the ladder and slide were located and where Josh was already attempting to mount the lowest rung. Two uniformed attendants were on *my* tail now, loudly ordering me to get off the course. I could hear laughter coming in waves from the stands. Perhaps the audience thought this was part of the evening's entertainment, a planned few minutes of comic relief.

But there was nothing comic about what Josh was doing. Handicapped by his short legs, he quickly realized the ladder-and-slide was out-of-bounds and wisely abandoned that obstacle. Instead, he headed for the first tunnel and made it through with flying colours. The zigzag, a challenge to bigger breeds, presented no problem. Enthusiastic applause from the audience inspired Josh to spin around and perform an encore. Once again he dashed through the zigzag, this time in the opposite direction.

At this stage of Josh's impromptu performance the judge, so queenly and composed up to this point, broke into laughter, at the same time dropping her program and notes, which tumbled into a disorganized heap at her feet.

The announcer's voice broke through the commotion. "Will the gentleman in charge of the Chihuahua kindly retrieve your dog without delay so we can get on with the event? *Please*!"

The two attendants were at my side now, one of them yelling, "Get that mutt out of here, kid, *now*!"

"He's *not* a mutt!" I yelled back.

"We don't care *what* he is. Just pick him up and get him out!"

Josh, the creator of all this mayhem, meanwhile was heading for the first of the fences. "Josh," I shouted, "no, *no*, you come. *Come, boy.*"

But Josh was in no mood to obey. This was his moment. Maybe he'd waited all his life, out there on Rebecca O'Hearn's estate, to demonstrate to the world that even a Chihuahua's grasp can exceed his reach.

Of course the fence was too high for him. A German shepherd might have cleared it with aplomb. But a Chihuahua? Not in a thousand years. But did it stop Josh? No. Taking a run, Josh leapt into the air. As he did, his body turned so that he slammed sideways into the upper beam and landed on the turf with a thud. Undaunted, he dashed back to where he figured he could take another run at the fence. Before he could begin his second run I managed to get within range of him. I took a flying leap — something I'd learned to do when I was taught how to steal home in Little League baseball. My outstretched hands caught Josh's hind legs and closed tightly around them, arresting his flight and bringing him to a full stop. Again the audience roared with amusement. Applause filled the air.

It was only when I got to my feet, Josh once again securely cradled in my arms, that I realized bulbs were flashing in our faces, Josh's and mine. And a television camera was fixed on us, its accompanying bank of lights forcing me to squint uncomfortably.

I heard a voice coming from behind the camera call out, "Hey kid, what's your name? What's the dog's name?"

Another voice said, "Where're ya from, kid?"

More flashbulbs were exploding in our faces. More shouted questions. Three security guards now, looking upset, were nudging us out of the ring.

Somebody in the stands nearby shouted, "Give the dog another chance!" Another person called out, "That pooch is the best act in the show. Put him back on."

Behind me now was a trail of people — the exhibition security guards, the television cameraman and his lighting assistant and three people with pads and pencils whom I took to be newspaper reporters.

One of the reporters, a young woman, catching up to me, grabbed my elbow.

"Please," she begged, "just tell me the dog's name and your own name. It'll make a wonderful piece for my paper."

"Let go of him, young woman," Gramps snapped.

I looked at the unhappy young reporter and shrugged. She looked at Grandfather. "Please, sir, all I want — "

"I don't care a hoot what you want," Grandfather said. "Get away."

The television crew followed on our heels as far as the nearest exit. Then, watching the three of us rush out through the revolving door, they abandoned their pursuit, but not before they'd succeeded in taking additional footage.

Back in the car, Grandfather turned and looked straight at me. "A fine mess you've made of things. Do you realize what's going to happen now?"

"No. What?"

"By eleven o'clock tonight we'll be on every television screen from Toronto to Timbuktu. There won't be a living soul in North America that doesn't know we're here. And it's all your fault."

"How was I supposed to know Josh would try a stunt like that?" I protested angrily.

"Dogs are only dogs, they never grow up. You should've known that. Dogs often do unpredictable things. They have to be closely watched. You should've known that, too. You fell down on the job. It's as simple as that."

I wanted to tell Gramps I hated him. Hated him and his perfectionism. Hated Rebecca O'Hearn for dying when she died, for not living at least long enough to sign her new will. Hated Hollis Burden for failing hours earlier to bring

Grandfather's escapade to a halt. Hated myself for choosing to spend the summer with him up at Port Sanford when other options were available. But above all, I wanted to tell him how, at that very moment, I would have given anything if somebody else — *any*body — was my grandfather.

And then it happened like the eruption of a volcano. I heard myself shouting at my grandfather, "I really hate you. I hate you, and I hate what you've gotten me into. I don't want this. I just want to go home."

"Hate is a luxury, a luxury you can't afford. The 'home' you want to go back to is no home. Your mother's thousands of miles away. And as for your father, well, need I say more? For better or worse you and I are stuck with one another. So whether or not you really hate me, you and I are going to have to make the best of it, at least for tonight."

As he said this, my grandfather pulled over to the first telephone booth he spotted after we had left the exhibition grounds. Switching off the engine, he said, "Wait here with the dog. I have to make a phone call. I'll only be a minute."

"You calling a hotel?"

"Of course not. Like I said, before the clock strikes eleven our faces are liable to be seen by everybody in this town who's sitting in front of a TV set and who is still awake."

"So where can we stay tonight?"

"You'll see."

"That's something else I hate," I said. "I ask you a question and all I get is 'You'll see.' Are you ever going to give me a straight answer to a straight question?"

Grandfather thought about it for a moment and then replied, "You'll see."

# Twenty-two

**W**e were travelling east along Queen Street, that was all I knew for certain, passing its intersection at Yonge Street, which by this time — it was now a little after ten — showed few signs of being the city's busiest. The sidewalks were deserted. In the windows of the department stores beautifully outfitted mannequins were wasting their fixed smiles on a scattering of penniless loiterers. Traffic was light at this hour. A few streetcars rattled by, their passengers leaning weary heads against the windowpanes, possibly heading to work on nightshifts at plants in the west end of the city.

We crossed Sherbourne and entered a part of Toronto — known to locals as Cabbagetown — that my parents had cautioned me to avoid, especially after dark. I could see now what they meant. Here and there, usually in the dim yellow light cast by some dingy little coffee shop, men slouched or squatted on the sidewalks, staring aimlessly at passing cars like ours. Some held in their hands brown paper bags, which they drew up to their mouths, tossing back their heads, drinking down whatever was concealed in the bags. My folks had told me it was usually some dirt-cheap wine that they'd managed to scrounge, or if a day of begging proved profitable the bag might contain a bottle of rum or whiskey. It occurred to me that some streets offered signs of life, but this section of Queen offered only signs of death. The men I was staring at, and who were staring back at me, seemed as lifeless as those mannequins back at Queen and Yonge.

I had heard the expression "no fixed abode" used in the news to describe men like these who got into trouble with the law. At this very moment, being driven to wherever my grandfather was taking me, I felt as though *I* had no fixed abode.

We kept travelling eastward. I sat in absolute silence wondering where on earth Gramps thought he was going. Josh, obviously exhausted, lay fast asleep next to me on the front seat of the old Buick. The immense grandstand of Woodbine Race Track loomed now and I recognized that we were approaching the area of Toronto called the Beaches. When I was younger and my mother and father were less consumed by their professions, I would be brought out to the Beaches for a stroll along the broad boardwalk that followed the shoreline of the lake for blocks. We would picnic in Kew Gardens, a generous well-treed patch of green that sloped gently down from Queen Street to the waterfront. The shops lining that stretch of Queen were small and operated mostly by middle-aged or elderly couples who looked to me as though they had been manufactured for the very purpose of running their modest establishments. I loved the Beaches then. The storekeepers and their places of business looked like Christmas cards even in summer.

Except for a handful of strollers, the sidewalks here were deserted too. The odd corner convenience store was still open. Otherwise all commerce in the area had been suspended till morning.

"Are you looking for a hotel or motel out here?"

"There *are* no hotels or motels in this part of town," came the curt reply.

"How would you know?"

"I know."

"How come you're so sure?"

"Trust me, I know."

"Then what're we doing out here in the Beaches?" I was getting testy.

"You'll see. Soon."

For a split second I saw the three of us driving off one of the steep cliffs just east of here, known as the Scarborough Bluffs, the old Buick hitting the deep waters of the lake and sinking like a giant stone to the muddy bottom.

"The least you can do is tell me where we're going," I said.

"The least *you* can do is trust me," Gramps said. "I'll say one thing for sure, it's pretty plain from what's gone on that you can trust me more than I can trust you."

He made an unexpected turn to the right and we were travelling south. I missed the street sign as we left Queen. "What street are we on now? Or is that a secret too?"

"Beech Street."

"Is that like B-E-A-C-H?"

"No, B-E-E-C-H … in case you're thinking of tipping off the police."

"Why would I want to tip off the police? Just because you've kidnapped your own grandson?"

Suddenly Grandfather pulled over to the curb. I figured that my last remark was the final straw, that he was going to toss me and my suitcase out on the sidewalk, wish me good luck and take off into the night with Josh as his silent lone companion. Instead he said quietly, "We're here."

"Where?"

"Here."

A porch light came on revealing a narrow two-storey house. Well, perhaps it was more like a cottage, with white clapboard siding, a blue door and blue trim around the windows and on the shutters. Someone at the living-room window, someone obviously keeping an eye out for us, disappeared and a moment later the front door was thrust open. A woman's voice called out, "What took you so long, Ira? I was beginning to think you'd gotten lost or something."

We got out of the car. "Bring Josh and your bag," Gramps said.

"Is this where we're spending the night?"

"Yes."

We mounted the steps to the porch. The woman gave grandfather a quick but affectionate kiss on the cheek. He returned the gesture. Nodding in my direction, he said, "Lena, this is my grandson, Benjamin Marshall."

The woman's face under the porch light was cheerful. "I'm very pleased to meet you, Benjamin — "

"Ben's good enough," I said.

"Ben it is," she said. "I've heard so much about you."

I was puzzled by this. "You have?" I said.

"Yes. I know you're — uh — thirteen?"

"I'll be fourteen soon."

"And you've been spending the summer up in Port Sanford with Ira. I bet that's been an interesting experience for a young man from Toronto." Her voice was pleasant, almost musical.

My response, I'm afraid, was hardly pleasant or musical. "It's been a real treat," I said.

"The lady's name is Mrs. Demarco," Gramps said.

The woman said quickly, "Please, Ben, call me Lena. 'Mrs. Demarco' makes me sound as if I'm my own mother."

She ushered us into the house.

Lena Demarco's home looked like the woman herself —

warm, immaculate, unpretentious. From the kitchen came the smell of fresh coffee.

"Ira," she said, "I baked some cinnamon buns, the kind you like. And don't worry about the coffee, it's decaffeinated. By the way, if you want to wash up or shower first, your robe and slippers are upstairs."

I set Josh down and looked straight at Grandfather as though I were seeing him for the very first time. I said, "Your robe and slippers are upstairs?"

For the first and only time in my memory, my grandfather was at a loss for words. He bit his lower lip, and stood looking awkward, shifting his weight from one foot to the other. At last, his eyes meeting mine with some difficulty, he said, "There's something I'd better tell you, Ben."

# Twenty-three

T he story my grandfather related — politely interrupted
from time to time by Lena Demarco to correct a date here
or a fact there — went like this:

It began in 1912 when he was in his final term at Osgoode
Hall Law School. One of the top students in his class, he was
selected to work as a law clerk at Elder, Wansborough and
Swann, a prestigious firm whose senior partners could trace
their family roots back a hundred and fifty years. He was being
groomed by Lewis Swann, the firm's chief litigator, for a
courtroom career. One day, in the not-too-distant future, the
name "Ira Lamport" was bound to show up prominently in
newspaper reports of important cases.

And then, during the final weeks of his clerkship at Elder,
Wansborough and Swann, the firm hired a young secretary for
its litigation department. Her name was Lena Mancini.

As my grandfather put it — and Lena Demarco agreed —
it was inevitable they would find themselves working together.

And that was when the trouble began. Serious trouble.
When Lewis Swann learned that his protegé was involved with
the young attractive Miss Mancini he summoned Grandfather
to his private office. "This will never do, Lamport," Swann
thundered. "We have a strict policy here at Elder and Company

against fraternizing between lawyers and the secretarial staff." His jowls shaking, the senior lawyer issued a stern threat. "Unless we have your word that you'll put an immediate end to this relationship of yours, I'm afraid we'll be obliged to dismiss the young woman. What's more, your own position here may have to be reconsidered."

Then, to make matters worse, Ira's parents as well as Lena's parents took strong objection to the young couple's love affair. Mother Lamport, a dyed-in-the-wool Scottish Presbyterian, faced the prospect of a Roman Catholic daughter-in-law with horror. "They'll twist your arm to sign your children over to the Pope, Ira, you just wait and see!"

Father Mancini was equally vehement. A devout Catholic, he painted a picture of hell and damnation if a union went ahead between his daughter and the Anglo-Saxon "cake eater." "You stick to your own people, Lena," her father advised. In the Mancini household, fatherly advice of that sort amounted to a decree. Any discussion was simply out of order. Nobody argued with the likes of Antonio Mancini. In his tiny world he was God.

"To make a long story short, Ben," Grandfather said, "I concluded that if the partners at Elder, Wansborough and Swann felt free to interfere with my personal life, then I didn't want any part of their organization. Everybody — my classmates, friends, parents and Lena, too — thought I was out of my mind when I told old man Swann what he could do with his high and mighty law firm and its policy. After my call to the bar, I went back up north and opened my own law office in Port Sanford. A year later, the First World War broke out. I volunteered, served as an artillery officer, was slightly wounded in France, sent back to England to recuperate, nursed back to health by a warm-hearted nurse from Edinburgh. We were married in a small church near the hospital in London just a week after the war ended. She was your grandmother, of course."

Lena Demarco said, touching my grandfather's forearm, "Let me take over Ira. It's late and poor Ben must be ready to drop."

Turning her attention to me, she went on. "I married a man by the name of Sam Demarco, a man my folks approved of. Actually, Sam was a dear sweet soul. We never had children, so I kept at my job as a legal secretary. Eventually I became office manager, not at Elder and Company but at an even bigger law firm. I retired about fifteen years ago. Soon after, Sam passed away. Later I read that Ira's wife — your grandmother — had also passed away. I think that was around the time you were born, right?"

"Right."

"So one day I found myself making a long-distance call. To this day I remember that my heart was in my mouth as I dialled the number. And then Ira came on the line."

Now it was Grandfather's turn again and his hand settled gently on Lena Demarco's forearm. Looking me straight in the eye he said softly, "We've been seeing each other regularly ever since. Usually down here, in Toronto, at Lena's house. So, you see, Ben, that's how come the robe and the slippers are upstairs."

I said, "Are you telling me now, Gramps, that all the years you've been bellyaching to us about how much you hate Toronto ... all the years you made excuses why you couldn't visit us more often or stay over once in a while ... all the years you pretended that your whole world was up there in Port Sanford ... you've been lying to us? Lying to Mom, lying to my dad, lying to *me*?"

Grandfather cleared his throat, letting go of Lena's hand at the same time. "Now hold on, Ben, it's not that simple." He reached out, intending to put a hand on my shoulder, but I drew back hastily. "Listen to me, Ben — "

"No, I won't listen," I said. "You told me I could trust you. You told me that time and time again. You even made me look like an idiot, first over that business with Hollis what's-his-name, and then over Josh getting loose at the dog show. Mr. Perfect, that was you. Mr. Dummy, that was me. Well, maybe I wasn't as smart as you, but at least I was honest."

"Let me explain, Ben. I didn't get to finish."

I rose from the table. "I don't want to hear any more. Anyway, why should I believe *any*thing you have to say? I mean nothing to you. I never did and I never will."

"Please, Ben," Lena said. "Sit down and let your grandfather explain — "

"Explain *what*? Just take me home, or at least let me go home on my own," I said. "I don't want to hear any more."

Lena, glancing at a clock on the kitchen wall, said, "Ben, it's getting on eleven o'clock. Spend the night here and I promise, if Ira can't or won't take you home, I'll deliver you to your doorstep myself. That's a promise."

"I don't know why I should trust your word any more than I trust his."

By now fatigue was working its way through my bones. My arms, empty as they were, felt as though they were shackled to lead weights. My feet felt as if they were nailed to the kitchen floor.

I thought, The worst thing about the life of a fugitive is that it's so *tiring*. I had no energy left to resist. "Okay," I said, "tonight, but that's *it*. First thing tomorrow, don't even bother with breakfast. Promise?"

# Twenty-four

In a well-tended stucco-and-brick bungalow in the city's north end, Harley Davidson, dog-tired after a long day on the roads, had sought lodging for the night with his cousin Pearl Langley and her husband Herb, a retired fireman.

It was a little past eleven and Port Sanford's Chief of Police, having gone that evening without supper, was hungrily pitching into a ham and cheese sandwich produced on short notice by his hostess.

All three were watching, with only mild interest, the late-night roundup of local news.

The program was coming to a close when Pearl Langley, yawning, moved to shut off the television set.

As she reached for the "Off" knob, Harley Davidson leaned forward, looking startled. "Hey, hold it!" he cried out, excited. "I want to see this — "

Pearl frowned. "Since when are you a fan of dog shows, Harley?"

"Since right now," Davidson said, breaking into a wide grin.

He shot up out of his easy chair, dropping part of his sandwich on Pearl Langley's polished oak floor. "I knew it, I knew it. I felt it in my bones!"

Heading quickly for the guestroom, he called back to his hosts, "I'm turning in for the night, but do me a favour and wake me up no later than six o'clock sharp. You know what they say: The early bird gets the worm."

# Twenty-five

"**B**en? Oh, Ben, are you awake?"

It was Lena Demarco's voice, drifting into my ears through the door of the spare room where I had bedded down for the night.

I threw on my pants and shirt and opened the door. Lena was standing there, a glass of orange juice in her hand. "Here, Ben, drink this down. It'll put sunshine into your day."

I accepted the glass of juice and followed Lena downstairs to the kitchen.

Gramps was already seated at the table. He put down his fork and sat staring down for a moment at a plate of uneaten eggs. Then he looked up at me. "Join me?" he said. "There's enough here for two, y'know."

"No, thank you," I said coldly.

I turned to Lena. "If it's not too much trouble, Lena, could I just have another glass of orange juice?"

"No, Ben, you can't," Lena said.

Thinking this must be a joke, this kind-looking soft-spoken woman couldn't be serious, I said, "I beg your pardon?"

She fixed her eyes sharply now on Gramps. "All right, Ira, there's a lot of unfinished business from last night." Then her eyes caught mine and held them fast. "Same goes for you, Ben."

She paused, looking first to one of us, then the other. "I'm waiting," she said in a no-nonsense tone. "Well, which of you is going to speak up first?"

There was a seemingly endless pause again. Grandfather looked down at his full plate. Without looking up he broke the silence. In a low voice, he said, "Have you any idea, boy, what it's like for a grandfather to be told that his grandson hates him?"

Looking straight at Gramps I said, "Have you any idea what's it's like to learn your grandfather's been lying for years and doesn't give a damn for his own flesh and blood?"

I rose from the table. "I left my suitcase in the living room. I'll just go get it, then I'm ready to leave."

I walked to the living room, leaving Gramps and Lena wordless at the table.

The living room drapes had been drawn wide open, admitting a brilliant early morning light. I went to the window and looked out at the small but neatly clipped lawn, and beds of impatiens planted on either side of the walk leading to a white picket fence. Just beyond was Grandfather's Buick parked at the curb.

I walked back to the kitchen.

"Funny," I said to Grandfather, "there's some guy looking over your car and writing something in a notebook, a guy in a cop's uniform."

"A police officer? My car?" He looked at Lena. "Since when do they hand out tickets for overnight parking on Beech Street?"

"They don't," Lena answered.

I returned to the living room, followed closely by Grandfather and Lena. "Look for yourself," I said, pointing to the officer now giving his attention to the three of us at the window.

"My God!" Grandfather said in a hoarse whisper. Quickly he moved to the front door of the house and threw it open.

"Harley?" he called out. "Harley Davidson? Is that you?"

"Morning, Ira," the officer called back, tipping his police cap politely. "Thought I might locate you here."

# Twenty-six

Josh had come out to the front porch of Lena's house. Planting himself at the top step like a miniature four-legged sentry, he was challenging the stranger down near Grandfather's car, yapping his head off, daring the large man in the police officer's uniform to move so much as one inch closer to us. Pretending to feel threatened, but unable to stifle a smile, Harley Davidson called out to us, "Will one of you please call off that beast! This here's the only uniform I own and I don't want him tearing it to shreds."

"Josh, shut up for God's sake," Grandfather yelled. What an unusual sight, I thought just then, a man barking at a dog! Looking over his shoulder at me, he said, "Ben, pick him up and put him in the house. He's already got us into enough trouble."

I did as my grandfather commanded, dumping Josh unceremoniously in the front hall, slamming the door on him and returning quickly to the porch.

"Harley, why're you here, and what's this all about?" Gramps said, eyeing the visitor suspiciously.

The Chief took a quick look up and down the street. "You want me to make a public announcement in front of the whole neighbourhood, Ira?"

With a curt motion, my grandfather beckoned the Chief

to approach. Standing now on the bottom step of the porch, Harley Davidson removed his cap. "'Morning, ma'am," he said to Lena. "Sorry to intrude on your privacy, but I've got some important business with Mr. Lamport." Looking over at me, he said, "Ira, I expect this is your grandson Benjamin Marshall, right? Fine looking lad. Looks a bit like you, Ira."

Despite the Chief's quiet manner and polite tone, Grandfather was in no mood for social pleasantries. Even more wary than before, he said, "I asked you why you've come here, Harley. I'm waiting for an answer."

Sidestepping around Grandfather's question, the Chief said to Lena, "And you must be Mrs. Demarco. I'm pleased to make your acquaintance, ma'am."

Lena looked stunned. How come this absolute stranger, the Chief of Police no less of some town a hundred and fifty miles away, knew her name? She began to say, "Have we met somewhere, Mr. … uh — "

"Lena," Gramps said, "let me handle this."

"But how does he know who I am?"

"I said, let *me* handle this, *please*."

Lena Demarco shrugged. "Oh, very well, Ira." The way she said this left no doubt in my mind that she was accustomed to giving in to my grandfather and letting him have his way. Did *any*one, I wondered right then, ever take on this cantankerous, headstrong old man and wrestle him to the mat?

I was about to find out.

"Well, Chief," Gramps said, sounding official and not at all friendly, "are you or are you not going to come to the point? What're you doing here this morning?"

The police officer looked embarrassed. "Aw c'mon, Ira, drop the 'Chief' stuff, will you? We've known each other ever since I was a kid delivering the *Port Sanford Echo* to your house."

"Am I under arrest, Harley? Is that what you're trying to say?"

"Ira, I know you're a lawyer and a darn good one, but please don't start cross-examining me. Just get your things together and we'll leave."

"I want to know, am I or am I not under arrest? And if I am, then what's the charge, Harley?"

Chief Davidson gave the same kind of shrug Lena had given. It wasn't exactly a sign of surrender, for the police officer gave no hint, standing there with his size twelve boots firmly rooted to the step, that he was about to back off. It was more a yielding of a very small patch of carpet to the older man before pulling the rug completely out from under him.

"Well, Chief, I'm waiting — "

"You're wanted back in Port Sanford," Davidson said calmly, "on suspicion of stealing a large but unspecified amount of money from the estate of Rebecca O'Hearn."

"On suspicion of what? — "

"I think you heard me the first time, Ira. Don't make me repeat the allegation. This isn't easy for me, you know."

"Who said I stole money from the old lady's estate? I'm entitled to know, Harley."

"Her three beneficiaries ... her niece and two nephews, that's who. Plus, they went out and hired Hollis Burden to track you down because *I* didn't believe the story at first. They must've promised him a slice of the pie if he managed to bring you back alive. For all I know, he's still tearing around this city in that crummy little Jeep of his, looking down open manholes and lifting the lids on garbage cans, especially if he saw the same television news I saw last night."

Looking intently into Harley Davidson's face, his voice no longer edged with hostility, Grandfather said, "Harley, do *you* think I'm a thief? You said you didn't believe the story at first. Does that mean you believe it now?"

"Ira, what I believe or don't believe is beside the point. I'm a police officer, not a judge. But I can tell you this: If I was a jury I'd have a tough time making up my mind about you. There's a mountain of ugly rumours piling up in Port Sanford about you and the boy and the dog running away like this. That's why you've got to come back. The sooner the better."

"Tell me something else," Gramps said to the Chief, narrowing his eyes so that no veil of secrecy could withstand that piercing gaze. "How did you know where to find me?"

Chief Davidson said, "I can answer that question in two words — Elsie Bjorklund. Elsie's had wind of your affair — " Here, the Chief hesitated for a moment, looked over at Lena and said, "Begging your pardon, ma'am — " Then he resumed lecturing Grandfather. "Like I said, Ira, smart as you are, you must've been deaf, dumb and blind, as they say, to keep that woman under your roof all these years."

"How could she possibly have known about Mrs. Demarco and me?"

Harley Davidson cast a nervous glance at Lena, then at me. "Maybe this isn't a fit subject to be discussing here in the presence of your grandson and the lady," he replied.

Gramps said, "Lena and I have known one another since long before you were born, Harley. And as for Ben, well, he's got to grow up sometime and now's as good a time as any. Go on."

"Well, you see, Elsie kept finding things around the house ... clues, maybe the odd envelope or bill or whatever, that made it pretty plain to her that you and Mrs. Demarco here were — "

Davidson paused, wondering whether he was overstepping

the bounds of discretion, waiting for some sign of permission to continue.

"Harley, for God's sake, go on," Grandfather snapped. "The summer'll be over and we'll still be standing here at this rate."

"I guess Elsie figured she had competition, so to speak. She became very jealous. No, more than jealous, she became downright angry. She told Agnes Trimble about you having a secret affair down here in Toronto but Agnes ordered her to keep her mouth shut. That's why the two of them never again exchanged a civil word between them. So, Elsie figured she had to tell *some*body."

"Who else in Port Sanford knows about this?" Grandfather demanded.

"Oh, no more than a handful, far as I know. Tom Bradley, the mayor, he mentioned he'd heard from his wife who runs into Mrs. Bjorklund at their hairdresser. And of course some of the guys at the barbershop know because it's next door to the hairdresser. Old Judge Kimber asked me one day a couple of years ago if I knew about you and your trips to Toronto, which meant, of course, that *he* knew, though I don't know who told him."

"Well, that settles it."

Chief Davidson said, "Settles what, Ira?"

"I've made up my mind, Harley."

Davidson's shoulders relaxed and he gave a smile of relief. "Good. Like I said, Ira, the sooner you get back to Port Sanford and deal with this matter head-on, the better. You must be tuckered out from all the driving you've done the last day or so. Maybe it'd be best if you drove back to Port Sanford with me."

Grandfather said, "You mean, in your police cruiser?"

"Yes."

"Like a prisoner?"

"No, Ira."

"Then why in your cruiser?"

Harley stalled a moment. "Well, you said you'd made up your mind, and I just want to make sure you don't have a last-minute change of heart."

"I don't think you understood me, Harley," Grandfather said. "I told you I'd made up my mind. And my decision is … I'm not going back, not with you, not with anybody. Not till I'm good and ready. I don't care about Rebecca O'Hearn's estate. I don't care about her stupid niece and her stupid nephews. And I sure don't care about the likes of Hollis Burden. I'm staying put, right here."

Harley Davidson's shoulders became tense once more. Quietly, looking very sober, he said, "I'm afraid that's not possible, Ira. Maybe you think you have a right to avoid your duty, but I can't avoid mine. Now, I'm asking you as a friend … an old and respectful friend … please get your stuff and come back with me. I'd like to hit the road and get back to Port Sanford by mid-day, no later."

Lena made a move as if to leave the porch. "I'll get your things together, Ira — "

"Don't bother," Grandfather said firmly. "I'm not going."

"But Ira — "

"Don't 'but Ira' me, Lena. I said I'm not going."

"But Gramps," I said, nodding in the direction of Harley Davidson down there on the step, "this man's a cop!" Then, thinking the word "cop" might be unflattering, I said hastily, "I mean, Chief of Police."

Not taking his eyes from the unhappy-looking police officer, Grandfather said, "I don't care *who* he is or *what* he is. I'm staying put."

Chief Davidson left the top step and mounted to the porch. "Suit yourself, Ira. Now then, I'm asking you once again to accompany me back to Port Sanford freely and voluntarily. If you refuse, I have no choice but" — here the Chief reached behind his own waist and unclipped a pair of handcuffs from a belt loop — "to cuff you and keep you under restraint until we're back up north in front of the judge. I hope I've made myself clear, Ira."

Neither man made a move. In the narrow space that separated them, the air seemed charged with electricity.

Lena touched Grandfather's arm. "Ira," she said softly, "you'd better do the right thing. Listen to the Chief."

"Nonsense," Grandfather retorted, but there was far less conviction in his tone now.

"In that case," the police chief said, his tone firmer now, "I'm obliged to handcuff you, Ira, and take you back forcibly."

Without losing another second, Harley Davidson stepped behind my grandfather. Efficiently, though not roughly, he drew the old man's long arms together and I heard the handcuffs click into place.

Chief Davidson gently nudged Grandfather down the steps and as far as the sidewalk. They moved past my grandfather's car to the Chief's cruiser, where the police officer opened a rear door. "Watch your head getting in, Ira," he said.

"Wait!" I heard myself calling out. "Wait!" I repeated, shouting this time. "I'm going, too."

At the open door of the Chief's sedan Grandfather had now drawn himself back to his full height. Looking down at me he said, "Why would you want to do a darn fool thing like this? You don't owe me anything, Ben."

"I'm not doing it for you," I said. "I'm doing it for me. I mean, how's it going to look to people, me just standing by while you get carted off to Port Sanford all by yourself?" I turned to Chief Davidson. "Can't you take off those hand-cuffs?" I asked.

"Nope, sorry," the Chief replied. "It's got to the point where I'm not sure I can trust your grandfather. Maybe *you* can. After all, blood's thicker than water, or so some folks say."

*Could* I trust Gramps? Mr. Cross-Your-T's and Dot-Your-I's? Mr. Perfectionist? The so-called stickler who decided strictly in his own mind not to carry out his client's instructions? The man who led a secret life and pulled the wool over the eyes of his own family? But then, if I didn't trust him now, who would?

"Okay, Chief," I said, "I'll make you a deal. If I come along, and Josh comes too, and I keep an eye on Gramps, will you remove the cuffs?"

The Chief eyed me warily. "I dunno. Why would a kid like you want to get mixed up in this mess?"

"I already said why. Besides — " I nodded in the direction of Gramps. "With those things on his wrists he looks like some crook in a chain gang. Would *you* want to see your grandfather looking like that, Chief?"

Chief Davidson took a long moment to consider my propo-sition. Then, shaking his head as though doubting the wisdom of what he was about to do, he unlocked the handcuffs. "All right, kid," he said, "go fetch that little yap machine you call a dog. I haven't got all day, y'know."

# Twenty-seven

So here we were at the Port Sanford County Courthouse. Harley Davidson, pulling his black-and-white sedan into the spot marked "Reserved For Chief of Police," announced that we were expected in the chambers of Magistrate McEwen, the local judge before whom criminal cases were heard. There the charges against Grandfather would be officially read out to him, he would be required to plead guilty or not guilty, and a date would be set for his trial.

But instead of shepherding us into the courtroom, the Chief made a detour and we were ushered into the magistrate's private office. Behind a seedy desk sat the magistrate, and the only visitor's chair in the small room was occupied, to our surprise, by Agnes Trimble. She sat stiffly, her back straight, her thin face showing signs of strain. At her feet was a large carton filled to overflowing with files and papers and a thick ledger.

Agnes was the first to speak. "Thank heaven you're back, Mr. Lamport. I've lost track of how many times your daughter has called from some town in the south of France near Nice. And your son-in-law — uh, I mean Dr. Marshall — well, I'd rather not quote him verbatim. I'll just say that he finally gave up calling and I believe he's on his way here to Port Sanford.

Perhaps you should try calling both of them as soon as possible. They sounded terribly upset."

"All in good time, Agnes," Grandfather said calmly, showing no sign that he was perturbed about my parents' apparent anxieties.

"Yes, all in good time, Miss Trimble," Magistrate McEwen chimed in. "First things first. We have some important court business to conduct."

The magistrate looked over in my direction, glaring. "You there," he called to me, "what's that … that *thing* you've got cooped up in your arms?"

"It's a dog, sir."

"Are you in the habit of bringing dogs into Her Majesty's courts of justice?" he asked, sounding irritable. "We're not running a circus, you know."

"I'm sorry, sir," I replied, "but this is the first time I've ever been in a courthouse or a judge's office."

"In that case," snapped the magistrate, "you've a lot to learn about the dignity of the legal system. Take that animal out of here, at once!"

"Begging your pardon, Mister — "

"My title is 'Your Worship,' young man. When addressing me you are to call me by my proper title."

I began again. "Begging your pardon, Your Worship, but this animal stays right here with me, and I stay right here with my grandfather."

"Ben," my grandfather said gently, "you'd better do as His Worship says." He gave me a rueful smile and a shrug that said there's nothing we can do about this.

I was unmoved. I said to my grandfather, "In court cases there are exhibits, aren't there, pieces of evidence that have to do with the trial?"

"Yes."

"Well, then, Josh here is a piece of evidence, which means he has every right to be in a courtroom or in a judge's office, which means we're staying right here, Josh and me."

As I uttered these last words I looked Magistrate McEwen right in the eye and we spent the next minute or so sizing up one another.

The magistrate was roughly the same age as Grandfather though less well preserved. His bushy moustache, stained yellow from tobacco, drooped over his upper lip like the fringe of a carpet that's been left out in the rain too many times. Behind thick bifocals his eyes squinted up at me as if I was some foreign substance that modern science had not yet succeeded in identifying. Fine red and black lines crisscrossed his bulbous nose, turning it into a roadmap. In the air of the stuffy office, besides mildew, there was a distinct odour of alcohol linked, I reckon, to the man's thick back-of-the-throat voice and wheezing noises that must have originated somewhere deep in his lungs. Yes, I thought to myself, I *am* learning a lot about the dignity of the legal system.

At last, Magistrate McEwen mumbled, "Oh, very well, young man, since you're obviously as pigheaded as your grandfather, stay if you must, but see to it that the creature doesn't interfere."

He squinted up at Gramps now. "Well, now, Ira, what have we been up to these last couple of days, eh?" he wanted to know, sounding like a school principal.

Standing erect before the magistrate's desk, his hands clasped behind his back, Grandfather resembled an errant pupil summoned to repent for some misdemeanour, except that his voice was firm, his tone unapologetic. "Chief Davidson informs me I'm to be charged with just about every crime known to the human race, Your Worship. I'd like to get on with it, then. I'd be grateful if we could proceed with the customary preliminaries so I can enter my plea of not guilty, arrange bail and retire to my home."

The magistrate and Miss Trimble exchanged knowing glances. "That won't be necessary, sir," McEwen said with sudden formality.

Grandfather looked first at the magistrate, then to Agnes, then turned and glanced at Chief Davidson. There was something peculiar going on here, something he didn't seem to understand.

Sensing my grandfather's confusion, the magistrate said, "You're a very fortunate man, Ira, maybe luckier than you deserve, if you don't mind my saying so. Miss Trimble here has presented me with all the facts I need to satisfy me, all the financial records etcetera in that box of papers concerning Rebecca O'Hearn's estate. There are no grounds, not a shred of evidence of guilty conduct."

Looking even more confused, Gramps scowled angrily at the chief of police. "Then what was all that baloney you gave me back in Toronto about fraud, theft — those were nothing but a bunch of trumped-up charges, weren't they, Harley?"

Magistrate McEwen pushed back his chair and got to his feet. "Now hold on, Ira and don't go blowing your top at Chief Davidson. He was only doing his duty. After all, your conduct *was* highly suspicious — "

Grandfather was aghast. "Highly suspicious!" He was barely in control of his temper now. Addressing the magistrate by his first name, he said, "Jack, we've known each other since college. I've never broken the law, not even *once* in my entire lifetime."

"That's not quite true," I said. "Down in Toronto you went through stop signs and red lights and disobeyed the speed limit signs more times than I could count. We're lucky to be alive."

My grandfather's face flushed with embarrassment, and Magistrate McEwen looked at me with a degree of interest he hadn't previously demonstrated. "Is that so, young man?" he said, sounding intrigued.

Warming to this particular subject, I replied, "Yes. And when I asked him why he didn't bother to come to a full stop he said 'Full stop is a phrase that's capable of many definitions.' Those were his exact words. He called it 'creative thinking'."

The magistrate's eyebrows shot up in his forehead. He seemed fascinated. "Go on," he urged. "What else did your grandfather teach you?"

Gramps suddenly began to cough loudly and I knew this was a signal for me to silence myself but I chose to ignore him. Of course, I was glad that he was innocent of the charges that he'd committed serious crimes, but there was just enough of a mean streak in me at this point that I wanted to see him squirm at the sound of his own words.

"Please," McEwen said to me, "continue with this business about — " he looked directly at my grandfather — "what did he call it ... creative thinking? I'm dying to hear more."

Grandfather's eyes were begging me to shut up and he was still coughing, though his cough had grown weak. Still, I carried on. "My grandfather says that what's written in the law books is one thing, but what's written between the lines is another."

The magistrate paused to digest this. "Well, well, well," he said slowly. He pursed his lips and looked grim, but somehow I had the feeling that he was trying to suppress a laugh, or at least a smile.

He sat down again behind his desk, but didn't take his eyes from my grandfather's. Shaking his head from side to side, looking up steadily at Gramps, he said in a voice tinged with sadness, "The things you learn about a person you've known most of your life … or *think* you've known."

Grandfather dropped all formality now. "Look here, Jack, those things I said to my grandson, I was only making conversation. You know how it is. Grandchildren sometimes pester you with questions and you have to satisfy their curiosity, so — "

"So," the magistrate said, interrupting, "you tell 'em how to go about breaking the law, do you? That's a fine example to set for youngsters."

I was waiting for Grandfather to even the score, bearing in mind that the strong smell of alcohol that surrounded the magistrate doubtless raised some interesting questions in the minds of *his* grandchildren. But here I learned something else about the dignity of the legal system. No matter how long lawyers and judges have known one another — or *think* they have known one another — there is a line that separates the man up there on the bench from the man down there at the counsel table. The plain fact is that the man up there on the bench is several feet closer to God and must be respected accordingly. So my grandfather, still reminding me of a student who'd been hauled into the principal's office, allowed himself to be chided by someone who was also less than perfect.

"I guess," the magistrate said, "deep down, people never really get to know each other, do they Ira? I mean, they never get to know each other a hundred percent. Parents and children, grandparents and grandchildren, husbands and wives, next-door neighbours, we rub shoulders every day, exchange greetings and gossip, live side by side and do business face to face. But every single one of us has some tiny locked cupboard that nobody can peek into, eh, nobody. You had us all plenty worried, Ira. Plenty upset and even scared, too. Well, it's over. You're free to go home, you and the boy, and be sure to take that dog with you. And one final thing, Ira — "

"Yes? — "

"Behave yourself."

The magistrate told us it was over. But he was wrong.

# Twenty-eight

It was one of those mornings — blue cloudless sky, gentle breeze, smell of damp early morning earth — when life seems normal again. We were relaxing, Gramps and I, on adjoining rockers on the front porch, awaiting Agnes Trimble's arrival and the start of my grandfather's first day back at his office.

On my lap sat Josh, flicking his ears like antennae to catch every sound that floated our way. Occasionally, sensing the approach of one or another of the neighbourhood dogs out on morning rounds, Josh would issue a warning growl. As far as he was concerned, Gramps' house was now *his* domain and any canine passerby, no matter how innocent, was a trespasser.

Three days earlier, after Magistrate McEwen had dismissed us and we had settled ourselves once again at my grandfather's house, I managed to connect with my father by telephone. He had just emerged from a lengthy session in the operating room and there was an unmistakable tension in his voice, as though he'd been in combat with some overpowering force of nature.

"Are you safe?" he wanted to know. "You're not in any danger?"

"Yes … and no."

"Very well, then. As soon as I finish my rounds later this afternoon I'll try to get away to pick you up. I never wanted you to get involved with your grandfather up there in Port Sanford, you know. It was entirely your mother's idea, Ben."

"That's not true," I said. "It was *my* choice."

"No point crying over spilt milk," my father said. "Get your things together and we'll have you back in the city in no time." There was a moment's pause, and then my father asked, "By the way, is there a bus you could possibly take back to Toronto? It would lift a lot of pressure off me today."

"I don't know what the bus schedule is," I replied. "Maybe Gramps knows." I looked over at Grandfather. He was standing nearby, pretending to be absorbed in a stack of mail that had accumulated during his absence, but I could tell by his expression that he had been eavesdropping and caught the gist of the telephone conversation. As always, my father's agenda came first, and nobody knew this better than my grandfather.

I said into the telephone, "I'm not coming back to Toronto, not yet anyway. I'm staying here, at least for the next few days, maybe longer."

"You could stay with me until your mother returns from wherever she is at the moment," my father said.

The offer sounded half-hearted at best. "No, thanks," I said. "I'm perfectly comfortable here."

"I understand there's a dog in the household."

"Yes, Josh, a giant Chihuahua."

"The one a lot of people saw on television a few nights ago — "

"Right."

"Well, be very careful, Ben. I can't count the number of rabies cases I've seen over the years. It's a miserable business, rabies. The victim has to get all sorts of shots, you know."

"Thanks for the advice, Dad. I'll try not to bite him."

"And be sure to check with your mother ... I mean about staying up in Port Sanford. You'd better clear that situation with her first."

"I'll call Mom right away," I promised, and hung up, not the least bit surprised that my decision to stay with Grandfather had earned my father's instant approval. He had always shown more patience toward his patients.

No sooner had I put down the phone than it rang. It was my mother calling long-distance.

"Where are you calling from? I just spoke to Dad and he didn't seem to know where you are," I said.

There was an angry edge to my mother's voice. "Nonsense. Of course he knows I'm in Nice. We've spoken several times over the last couple of days. Ben, what on earth did you and your grandfather think you were doing? You had us worried sick."

"'Us'? Who's 'us'?"

"Your father and me, of course. Who else?" Though she was thousands of miles away, I could feel her temperature rising.

"It's nice to know," I said, "that you and Dad finally got to agree on something."

"Don't get smart with me, Ben. I'm in no mood for jokes. I want you back in Toronto where you belong."

"Back with who?"

"You mean *whom*." She was forever editing my English. "Back with your father ... mind you, it's just until I return from France, Ben."

"And how soon will that be?"

"Two or three weeks, I hope. I still have a load of research to complete."

"Uh huh. Two or three weeks."

"Ben? Are you still on the line?"

"Yes."

"You *will* go right back to Toronto, won't you, dear? I don't think your grandfather is in any condition to — "

"No."

"Pardon?"

"I said no, Mom. I'm not going back, not until I'm good and ready."

Her voice hardening again, my mother said, "Ben, I want to speak with your grandfather. Put him on the line, please."

"He just left," I lied. "He has a case in court and he was late."

"Then let me speak to Mrs. Bjorklund, Ben."

"Mrs. Bjorklund's gone," I said.

"Gone? What do you mean, gone?"

"I mean gone. Gramps did what the chief of police told him to do. He fired her … this morning."

"I don't understand, Ben. Mrs. B. had been with your grandfather more years than I can remember."

"I'll explain everything when you get back from France, Mom."

"Then who's taking care of your grandfather? Who's looking after the house? My God, Ben, what's happening up there? Have you all gone crazy?"

"We haven't gone crazy, and Lena is looking after Gramps and the house. I mean, she's going to when she gets here a few days from now."

"Lena? Who is Lena? Do I know her?"

"No, I don't think you know her. She's Grandfather's girlfriend."

"*Girl*friend! Ben, what're you talking about? Your grandfather hasn't got a girlfriend. Have you been getting into his Scotch? Have you been dipping into your grandfather's liquor supply? Are you drunk, Ben? I want the truth, young man."

"The truth is, Mom, I've got to go. I'm looking after the

house till Lena … Lena Demarco's her full name … till she arrives. I've got a million-and-one things to do, so I'm gonna say goodbye now. G'bye, Mom."

My grandfather was giving me one of his stern looks of disapproval. "I lost count of the number of lies and half-truths you just told your mother, Ben," he said, shaking his head from side to side.

But I could tell he was smiling. Not one of those smiles you can see. One of those smiles that lies sandwiched between a person's outer skin and his skull. You can't see it, but you know it's there.

Shading his eyes from the sun beating down, Grandfather rose from his rocker and pointed to a dark sedan coming up the street. "Ah, good, that must be Agnes." He seemed impatient, as though he could scarcely wait to get back to work. "That's not her car. I wonder who's giving her a lift — "

The sedan pulled into Grandfather's driveway and Gramps took a couple of steps forward to greet his secretary.

But the first person to get out of the car wasn't Agnes Trimble. From the driver's side a young man in his mid-thirties emerged. He was very trim, wearing a seersucker summer jacket, a white shirt with a neatly patterned necktie, grey slacks and well-polished shoes. Somehow he didn't strike me as a person who lived in Port Sanford.

A moment later another man got out of the car, this time from the front passenger's seat. His clothes looked slept in. If it hadn't been for some kind of badge pinned to his ill-fitting blue serge jacket, I'd have taken him for a panhandler. His shoes looked as though they'd been in a war.

Both men took a few steps toward the porch but it was obvious that they were moving with a certain degree of caution. The younger one, the well-turned-out fellow, looked nervous and uncomfortable. The other, grim at first, suddenly broke into a grin revealing a need for extensive dental work. "Well, Ira," he called out, keeping a safe distance, "we meet again. History has a way of repeating itself, doesn't it? Or, as they say, what goes around comes around." The man wore a self-satisfied smile on his poorly shaven face.

Grandfather moved closer to the steps. "If you have any more clichés in your repertoire, I wish you'd write them down for me, Hollis," he said. "I may want to quote them ... when I'm in a mood to bore people to death."

Hollis Burden's smile evaporated. Jerking his thumb in the direction of the man accompanying him, he said, "This here's Mr. Simon Connybear, of Hudson, Millard and Connybear, one of them big law firms down in Toronto. Mr. Connybear's a specialist in handling estates."

The man in the seersucker jacket cleared his throat. "Good morning, Mr. Lamport," he said. His manner was polite, respectful. "I'm sorry to intrude like this but — "

"But," Hollis Burden cut in, eager to be the bearer of bad news, "Mr. Connybear's got a court order from Judge Kimber that says he's *in* and you're *out*."

Grandfather frowned. "He's in and I'm out? Meaning what?"

The younger visitor suddenly found the courage to step forward and take over. Still speaking politely, Connybear said, "My law firm has been retained by the beneficiaries of Rebecca O'Hearn's estate. In view of their differences with you and ... uh ... your recent unanticipated ... .uh ... shall we call it your *departure*? ... we were obliged to obtain an order from His Honour Judge Kimber on an urgent basis ... an order removing you as executor and trustee of Mrs. O'Hearn's estate, and appointing — " He cleared his throat, loudly this time. " — appointing me in your place." Connybear reached inside his jacket pocket and removed and unfolded a document with an official-looking blue back. "I have a copy of the judge's order for your records."

The young lawyer took another step in Grandfather's direction and was about to hand over the document when Hollis Burden unceremoniously grabbed it out of his out-stretched hand. "I'm here from the Sheriff's Office to see to it that this order gets enforced according to the letter of the law, Lamport," Burden said, adding with a sneer, "You know all about the letter of the law, I presume?"

"*I* certainly do, Mr. Burden," Gramps said. "I'm not too sure about *you*, though."

Swallowing this latest insult, Hollis Burden carried on. Sounding like the town crier, he read aloud from the document:

> The said Ira Lamport is hereby ordered forthwith to yield and deliver up all property in his custody and pos-session belonging to or having to do with the estate of the deceased Rebecca O'Hearn, including without lim-itation all books of account, financial and legal records, funds on hand in trust for the deceased's estate, and any and all other property of every kind and description whatsoever.

He raised his eyes from the paper. Again with a sneer, he said to Gramps, "Would you like me to repeat this for you?"

Quietly Gramps replied, "Only if you're anxious to demon-strate something we never knew before, namely that you can actually *read*."

"Mr. Connybear's a very busy man and his time is valu-able, so let's get on with it. My duty, Ira, is to see to it that you hand over to this gentleman here everything that's covered by the court order ... and I *do* mean everything. And there's to be no disturbance of the peace, if you take my meaning, Ira. Don't you go off half-cocked and do something foolish like you done a coupla days back. We're not about, Mr. Connybear and me, to put up with any nonsense."

Nodding solemnly, Grandfather said, "I understand perfectly." "May I," he said, addressing the lawyer, "have the courtesy of examining that copy of Judge Kimber's order before we proceed?"

Connybear replied, "Of course, sir," and motioned to Hollis Burden to hand the paper up.

With his bifocals perched precariously at the tip of his nose, my grandfather inspected the document, giving it what struck me as microscopic scrutiny. Snorting, he mumbled, "Don't they teach judges nowadays how to punctuate? These clauses oughta be separated by semi-colons, not commas. Shameful! Disgraceful!"

Gramps turned to me. "Ben, you know that carton — the one that Agnes took down to the Magistrate's chambers, with all the files and papers — it's back now in my office." His voice was composed but his tone was one of resignation, even defeat. "Can you manage to fetch it out here, please?"

The container was heavy and I handed it over to Connybear with a sense of relief.

Grandfather said to Simon Connybear, "There's a good many years of legal work in that box, sir. No doubt you may have some questions as you go through the files. Feel free to call upon me if you require any assistance."

"That's very good of you, Mr. Lamport," Connybear responded. "I appreciate your offer, sir."

Hollis Burden touched the young lawyer's sleeve. "Now hold on a minute," he said, "I wouldn't rush to take Lamport up on his offer of help. He's a tricky guy. Besides, he's pretty unstable, if you ask me." Looking up at Grandfather, Burden asked, "The money, Ira … what did you do with the money?"

"What money?" Gramps said.

"C'mon, Ira, I'm talking about all the money that was in the old lady's bank account when she kicked the bucket."

With astonishing composure, Grandfather said, "Let's get three things straight, Burden: Number one, never ever again in my presence refer to Rebecca O'Hearn as 'the old lady.' Number two, Rebecca did not, as you so crudely put it, kick the bucket; she passed away. Number three, if you look at the banking records which we presented to Magistrate McEwen you will see that I have exactly a hundred and three dollars and eighty-one cents of Mrs. O'Hearn's sizeable fortune in my possession. It's in a trust account and you have my word as a lawyer and a gentleman that I will forward a cheque this very day to Mr. Connybear's law firm for that full amount."

The sheriff's deputy looked disappointed. "What else you got, Ira, that belongs to the estate? You expect me to believe that's all there is, this box fulla stuff and a lousy hun'red'n three bucks?"

"That's *it*," Grandfather said.

There was a skeptical expression on Hollis Burden's face, but suddenly a wily smile took over. "There's one thing you forgot, Ira," he said.

"I'm not aware that I've overlooked anything — "

"Oh yes, you have," Burden said, sounding as though he was teasing.

"I don't know what you're referring to, Hollis."

"The dog, Ira. I'm referring to the dog."

"What about the dog? — "

"He's the property of the estate. The court order said all other property of every kind and description whatsoever. You want me to read it to you again? That includes the mutt. You gotta hand him over now."

I glanced at Simon Connybear. The look on his face told me the last thing in the world this lawyer wanted to transport back to his office in Toronto was a ten-year-old Chihuahua.

The Sheriff's deputy mounted the steps to the porch, moving more boldly now but keeping a sharp eye on my grandfather, on the lookout for any sudden threatening motion. A space of five or six feet was all that separated him from where I was seated holding Josh. That's when Josh erupted, barking as if some kind of alarm had just gone off inside him.

"Can't you shut that animal up?" Burden said, keeping his distance. Over his shoulder he called to Simon Connybear, "Don't you worry, Mr. Connybear, if I have to, I'll go get a cage."

Grandfather stepped between Burden and me. "Maybe there'd be less of a fuss if my grandson carries the dog down to Mr. Connybear's car."

Burden said, snarling, "I don't give two hoots how we get the mutt outta here. Let's just not take all day to do it."

Rising from my rocker, still cradling Josh, I said to my grandfather, "I can't believe this is happening."

"Can't believe *what* is happening?"

"That you're actually giving up like this … no argument, no plea for mercy, nothing. Somebody snaps their fingers and it's so long, Josh, nice to have known ya."

"You don't understand, Ben," Grandfather said. "This isn't a case of somebody simply snapping their fingers. These people arrived armed with a court order."

"You're right, I don't understand, not one bit. You spared Josh's life the morning you took him to the vet and then brought him right back. Mrs. O'Hearn's will said Josh was to be put down after she died, but your conscience wouldn't let you go through with it. And now — "

"That's enough, Ben!" Grandfather shouted. "I made a mistake once by putting my personal feelings above my duty. I'm not going to make the same mistake again. Take Josh down to Mr. Connybear's car at once. For all of our sakes, let's get this sorry business over and done with. Do it *now*!"

Without letting go of Josh I said, "Okay, but I'd better get his leash. They're going to need it to make sure he doesn't get loose."

Gramps looked at me curiously. "Leash? What leash? I don't recall Mrs. Tidy bringing any leash."

"Oh yes, she did," I said. "It's up in my room. Maybe you forgot. I never used it because Josh is so small I figured we wouldn't need it. But after what happened at the dog show, he'd better be kept on a leash, that's for sure."

"All right," Burden said, "but make it snappy, kid. Like I said, we haven't got all day."

Holding Josh securely in my arms, I said, 'I'll be back in a flash."

I turned and went into the house. I went directly to the kitchen, to the rear door of the house. The door opened onto a wooden stoop where I stored my bicycle. Attached to the handlebars was a deep wire basket. Slipping off my light summer jacket, I spread it at the bottom of the basket, transforming it into a mattress, and placed Josh down on it. "Lie down, boy," I said softy, "lie down, stay still and, for God's sake, don't made a sound!"

We took off, Josh and me, down the rear steps. Across the backyard we raced. Through an opening in the picket fence. Into the lane that ran along the back of the houses on Grandfather's block. Onto the first street south. Standing on the pedals, I was pumping for all I was worth. Down one street, along another, block after block, looking neither to my left or my right but straight-ahead. Almost before I knew it, I was at the edge of town. I turned onto the service road that led to the main highway, making great time. Wind filtered through the wire mesh of the basket, fanning Josh's face, forcing his eyes to blink and his nose to twitch.

A familiar billboard came into view as the service road met the shoulder of the main highway. In white letters against a royal blue background it announced: YOU ARE NOW LEAVING PORT SANFORD, CANADA'S FRIENDLIEST COMMUNITY. On the line below it said, this time in red letters: COME BACK SOON.

"Don't count on it," I said to myself.

Beyond the billboard was a road sign informing me that Toronto was a hundred and fifty miles away. I was pumping steadily, not coasting even on the occasional downgrade in the road, and keeping up the pace whenever confronted by hills which, fortunately, were few and far between and never all that steep.

I hadn't the faintest notion how I would ever get to Toronto, how long it would take, or what I would do when, by some miracle or incredible luck, we reached the city.

But it didn't seem to matter. What I was doing seemed so right. And what they were doing ... meaning Hollis Burden and Simon Connybear and, yes, my grandfather too ... seemed so wrong.

Another road sign appeared: *Toronto 140 miles*. I'd covered ten miles already! I had the feeling that I could go on and on, that there was a dynamo deep inside me churning electric energy directly into my legs.

I reached the sign that read *Toronto 125 miles*. Fifteen miles had flown by. But now the dynamo inside me was running out of fuel. Instead of blood, lead was flowing through the arteries and veins in my legs. My calf muscles felt as though iron fingers were closing around them, gripping tighter and tighter with each downstroke on the pedals. Every dip in the road, no matter how shallow, came as a blessing, an opportunity to coast if only for a minute or two. Every hill, no matter how gentle, presented a challenge. Maybe this whole exercise is stupid, I said to myself. Maybe I should turn around, go back to Port Sanford and simply hand Josh over to those two men, Burden and Connybear. And if I act really humble and apologize all over the place, or plead insanity, or tell them I come from a broken home, they'll take pity on me and on Josh. They'll smile and say "Aw, that's okay, kid, we understand. All of us make crazy mistakes." And then we'd all go over to Millie's Cornerstore for a milkshake, just like in the movies.

But that face kept coming to me, the face of Hollis Burden. I could hear his voice as he ordered me around as though I was some juvenile delinquent in a reform school. And I realized I must be dreaming if I thought there was even *half* a chance that an apology from me would do anything to change his mind about Josh. Anyway, what to do about Josh wasn't the real question. The real question on my mind was: Where was the courageous fighter, the champion, that Mrs. Tidy had described that day I sat with her in the O'Hearn kitchen and she told me how Gramps had saved her from ruin? Where was the man who took such wild chances when we were fleeing through the busy streets of Toronto, obeying the law one moment, breaking the law the next? I had expected my grandfather to stand up to Burden, to tell Connybear where he could shove the blue-backed court order he took from his pocket, to defy the final demand that Josh be turned over together with the box of files to the new lawyer for the O'Hearn estate. I had expected Grandfather to act like a hero. Instead, all he did was raise a white flag.

Go back to Port Sanford? No. God only knew how and when we would make it to Toronto, me and Josh and this creaking, squeaking two-wheeler under me. But turn around and go back? No!

I was approaching the first really difficult-looking hill, a long, steep and winding grade, when I heard the first blast of a car horn. It sounded as if it was coming from some distance behind me, but as it continued it became louder and louder. I turned my head to look over my shoulder, still pedalling as hard as I could but making slow progress as I started up the hill.

The car was closing in fast. In a moment it drew even with me, its shiny black fenders gleaming under the high morning sun, its white body almost blinding, the red and yellow lights on its roof rotating with that sense of emergency that is peculiar to police cruisers.

The window on the front passenger's side was open and I recognized the driver.

Shouting at me through the open window, Chief Harley Davidson said, "Pull over and stop, son. This is the end of the line."

# Twenty-nine

The trip had come to a sudden end. But, my troubles didn't.

Once again I found myself, with Josh keeping me company, being transported back to Port Sanford in a police cruiser. Same cruiser, same driver as last time.

Once again I found myself standing before Magistrate McEwen, his reddish face puffy and raw, as though he'd shaved with a sheet of coarse sandpaper. The difference this time is that I was standing in the magistrate's courtroom instead of his private office.

It was a Wednesday, the day of the week when juvenile offenders were tried for all sorts of crimes. Sitting in court waiting for my case to be called, I watched the cream of Port Sanford's young wrongdoers mumbling excuses as to why they'd broken into somebody's convenience store to steal cigarettes, or scrawled dirty words on tombstones in the local cemetery, or taken a bike that didn't belong to them or, worse still, made off with somebody's car for a so-called joyride. Each and every one had been caught red-handed and found guilty. Some were let off with a stern lecture and threats of jail terms if they reappeared in this court. Some were ordered to pay fines, which meant their parents would have to lay out hard-earned dollars. The joyrider was sentenced to reformatory for six months because it was his second conviction. Old McEwen had obviously got up on the wrong side of the bed that morning.

And then it was my turn to stand trial. The court clerk, a dangerously overweight man with an expression of boredom in his eyes and a note of boredom in his voice, rose from his station to read the charge. "Benjamin Marshall," he droned, "you are charged that on the twenty-second day of July, nineteen hundred and sixty-two, you did wilfully and unlawfully steal or cause to be stolen certain property belonging to the estate of one Rebecca O'Hearn, deceased, to wit ... a dog. To this charge, how do you plead?"

I looked at the clerk, then up at the magistrate. It was clear from their faces that they wanted nothing more than to hear me utter one word and one word only: "Guilty." My case could then be disposed of with as little muss and fuss as possible. The clerk could make a beeline for the Kozy Korner and lunch. As for Magistrate McEwen, he could make a beeline for his private office and *his* favourite luncheon, which came in a bottle.

I glanced briefly at Grandfather who was defending me, sitting just to my right. He nodded. Then I said, clearing my throat first, "Not guilty, Your Honour ... I mean, Your Worship, sir."

The clerk looked away, thoroughly disgusted. Magistrate McEwen's eyes narrowed and he shrivelled up his bulb-like nose. (You'd have thought that I'd just insulted his mother.) "Would you care to repeat your response to the charge?" he boomed. "Perhaps you misunderstood," he said, sniffling.

A bit louder, I repeated, "Not guilty."

Coughing longer than I thought necessary, the magistrate leaned forward over his desk, the deeply carved ruts in his brow knitted into a furious scowl. Aiming his wooden gavel in my direction as though it was a weapon, he sputtered, "Now look here, young man — " His voice was thick, and his words sounded as if they were being squeezed out through a narrow watery passage in his chest. "You would be wise to reconsider your plea. I'm telling you now that if you plead not guilty and, if I find you guilty, it's going to go very hard for you. I'll not stand for any nonsense in my court, and furthermore — "

Before the magistrate could finish his sentence my defender shot to his feet shaking with rage. "How dare you!" he yelled at the magistrate. "How *dare* you attempt to intimidate my client into changing his plea!"

Glaring down from the bench, McEwen shouted back, "How dare *you* address the court in this manner! Sit down, Mr. Lamport. One more outburst from you and I will not hesitate to hold you in contempt of court. I would have expected that a counsel with your experience would have more sense."

"And I would have expected that a magistrate with *your* experience would have some sense of justice," Grandfather shot back, still shaking.

"Let me remind you," McEwen said, his voice rising steadily, "that your client was apprehended by no less an officer of the law than the Chief of Police himself. What's more, the charge laid against your client was based upon information furnished by a sheriff's deputy. Therefore, Mr. Lamport, you and your client are shamefully wasting the valuable time of this court!"

"And let me remind *you*, sir, that no matter how a person happens to be arrested, he is presumed innocent until proven guilty beyond a reasonable doubt after a fair trial. It is *you*, therefore, who are shamefully wasting the valuable time of this court!"

"You are rude and impertinent, Mr. Lamport. I order you to sit down."

"I will *not* sit unless and until I have Your Worship's assurance that my client will receive a fair hearing. Otherwise,

I will insist that you relieve yourself of this case and assign it to another magistrate."

The magistrate's face was as close to purple at this point as any human face I've ever seen. Almost screaming, he replied, "You are arrogant beyond imagination, Mr. Lamport — "

Grandfather retorted, "And you are equally incompetent —"

The magistrate's gavel came down on his desktop like a sledgehammer. "That's *it*! I find you in contempt of court, counsel."

Shading his eyes from the glare of the overhead lights, the magistrate searched the courtroom. "Chief Davidson," he called out angrily, "where are you?"

From the rear of the crowded courtroom came a faint reply. "Here, Your Worship."

"Come forward," the magistrate barked.

Looking unhappy, Chief Davidson slowly made his way to the front of the court.

"Chief Davidson, I order you to escort Mr. Ira Lamport from this courtroom to a place of detention in this courthouse where he is to remain in custody until a decision as to a suitable penalty is made."

"But Your Worship — " Harley Davidson began to protest.

"Don't argue with me, Chief, or I may be forced to find *you* in contempt as well."

Slowly, awkwardly, Chief Davidson moved to Grandfather's side. "Ira, for God's sake," he whispered, "tell the old buzzard you're sorry."

"Not a chance, Harley," Grandfather said.

"*Please*, Ira, I'm begging you. Don't make me do this."

Grandfather shook his head. "You do what you have to do, Chief."

Silently, the two men shuffled toward the exit.

I called out, "Gramps, where are they taking you?"

Gramps stopped, turned and looked at me, smiling. "Don't you worry, Ben, it's just a lock-up down in the basement."

"Then I'm going, too," I said.

The court clerk suddenly moved close, as if to restrain me.

Impatiently Magistrate McEwen hissed, "Let the kid go with the old man, Clerk. I want them both out of my sight."

And so Grandfather and I found ourselves residing together in much closer quarters than we were accustomed to. We were sharing a bleak windowless cell in the courtroom basement next to the boiler room, occupying a rough wooden bench, watching the free world go by from behind a row of iron bars. Grandfather was sitting calmly, his arms folded across his chest, his back against the cool stone wall. His eyes were closed but I could tell he was lost in thought, not slumber.

There was a tremor in my voice as I asked my cellmate, "Gramps, how long can they keep us here? Will we ever get out?"

"Hand me my briefcase, Ben," he said. Extracting a yellow legal pad, he began vigorously to scrawl some sort of message in large letters, finishing with the words which he pronounced aloud as he wrote them: "Yours very respectfully, Ira Lamport, Barrister and Solicitor."

With an air of determination, Grandfather rose from the wooden bench and approached the bars of the cell. "Officer," he called to the police constable seated just outside the lock-up, dozing. The police officer sat up with a start. Grandfather dangled the sheet of paper between two of the bars, his long arm extending into the corridor.

"What can I do for you, Mr. Lamport?" the police officer said.

Grandfather motioned to the constable to come right up to the bars. The two men began to speak to each other almost in a whisper. The only words I could make out were "telegram," "urgent," "without delay." I saw Gramps dig into his pants pocket and slip something to the officer.

A moment later the officer disappeared down the corridor, the page from the legal pad neatly folded and tucked in the pocket of his tunic. I figured the bill was neatly stashed in his shirt pocket, close to his heart.

"What was all that about?" I asked, as Grandfather took his seat beside me on the bench.

"Oh," he said slowly, "I was just placing our dinner order for tonight. Something to go with the bread and water they usually serve around here."

Then he gave me a sly wink. "Better try and get some rest, boy. It's going to be a long day."

# Thirty

They forgot to bring us lunch that day as Gramps and I sat in the courthouse lock-up and around three o'clock in the afternoon — by which time the two of us were beginning to hear our stomachs rumble — Chief Harley Davidson showed up apologizing all over the place for the oversight. "Jeez, Ira," he said, sounding like a kid who forgot to do his homework, "you'll have to excuse us. I plumb forgot to arrange some food. Fact is, this is a whole new experience for me and my men. I mean, in all my years on the force this is the first I ever saw a lawyer cited for contempt of court and locked up. God knows, I've seen plenty of *clients* sitting there on that wooden bench, but you're the first *lawyer*."

Gramps, I thought, was amazingly gracious under the circumstances. "Well, now, Harley," he said, "don't you go agonizing too much just because my grandson and I happen to be starving to death down here. An old man like me can live off my own body fat for a day or two if I have to; it's really Ben here I'm concerned about. So, have you by any chance arranged for some sandwiches and coffee? If old McEwen means to keep us in this dungeon until they build a scaffold to hang us, a little refreshment would ease the pain, y'know."

I could see that the Chief had arrived empty-handed and now he was nodding soberly. I pictured my grandfather and me tearing at a dried crust of bread and taking turns at a glass of murky water later in the day before settling down for an uncomfortable night on that bench.

"Sorry, Ira," said Chief Davidson, "but I'm afraid you and the kid are going to have to look after your own eats."

My grandfather looked displeased. "Now how in the devil are we supposed to do that, Harley? We don't have the wings of an angel, man. We can't exactly fly through these bars. Besides, we've got a dog back at the house needs looking after."

"Don't worry about the dog," Chief Davidson said. "Agnes Trimble is looking after him. I called her before I came down here. Know what she said, Ira?" The Chief chuckled to himself. "She said isn't it ironic that the dog's in better shape right now than you and the kid! A dog's life isn't so bad after all, is it?"

Gramps' patience (which has never existed in an unlimited supply even at the best of times) ran completely dry at this point. "Harley," he said sharply, "save the philosophy for your next guests. Are you, or are you not, going to bring us something to eat and drink before we rot down here?"

"Sometimes, Ira, you don't listen as carefully as you should," Chief Davidson said. "I just told you — you're gonna have to fetch your own food."

A wry smiled creased Chief Davidson's face as he withdrew a piece of paper from his pocket and handed it through the bars to my grandfather.

Gramps was in no mood now for joking. "What's this?" he said, gruffly.

"A telegram. Read it, for God's sake, Ira — "

Clearing his throat, Gramps read the telegram aloud.

To Magistrate James C. McEwen:

It has come to my attention that a serious denial of natural justice has occurred in your court whereby an accused person, namely one Benjamin Marshall, was admonished to plead guilty to an alleged offence and threatened with severe consequences if he failed to do so. This forewarning was issued before any evidence was presented. Furthermore, upon your conduct being challenged by defence counsel for the accused, you saw fit to cite the lawyer for contempt of court and placed him under arrest, while at the same time confining his client who had not yet been convicted of a criminal act. Your actions regarding the juvenile Benjamin Marshall and his legal counsel Mr. Ira Lamport amount to breaches of their fundamental rights under our law. I order you accordingly to direct that these persons be released forthwith from custody. Moreover, at the earliest opportunity you are to make an apology to Mr. Lamport and his client in open court, in order to restore the integrity of our system of justice.

Yours respectfully, Wishart J. Arthurs

Attorney General for the Province of Ontario

"Well, Ira, don't go looking so surprised," said Chief Davidson. "After all, you didn't expect the Attorney General to ignore *your* telegram, did you?"

Grandfather played dumb. "*My* telegram? I don't know what you're talking about, Harley."

"The telegram you gave my officer guarding your cell. Well, he brought it to my office to get permission to send it. Actually,

I'm the one who sent it off to Toronto." With that, Chief Davidson took a ring of keys from his pocket, thrust a huge skeleton key into the lock, threw open the door and out we walked. We were free!

"Oh, and by the way," Davidson said, "here's your change from the twenty-dollar bill you gave my man. Buy yourself and the kid a couple of hamburgers with it."

The magistrate's apology was a stiff, cold, formal affair that took place next morning before a packed courtroom. His words sounded as though they had been chilled overnight in a deep-freeze. "It is my duty," he intoned, not looking at us, but glueing his eyes on the backs of his liver-spotted hands as though he'd never inspected them before, "to extend the regrets of this court."

The charge of theft that Hollis Burden had laid against me was withdrawn by Chief Harley Davidson that same morning.

Simon Connybear delivered a letter to Grandfather abandoning any claim to Josh, a move that surprised neither Grandfather nor me. This cleared the way for me to take Josh back to Toronto, where he now resides in our new apartment, taking up little space. The highlight of his dog day comes every morning around eleven when the letter carrier squeezes our mail through the slot in the front door and Josh uses his tongue, his tonsils and his lungs, and whatever other resources a six-pound Chihuahua can employ to keep strangers in a state of terror.

Lena Demarco has begun spending more and more time up in Port Sanford where she has succeeded in getting Gramps to, first, purchase his first new suit of clothing in ten years from Tom Yardley's Men's Wear, second, at least *think* about trading in the old Buick for something that doesn't sound like it's infected with tuberculosis every time you turn the key, third, strip the wallpaper in the house and paint the walls a cheerful shade of yellow, and, fourth, propose marriage.

Grandfather admits that the loss of the O'Hearn estate as a client means a significant reduction in his future income — a fact that can't be treated lightly. However, that fact hasn't stopped him from enjoying his nightly shot of Scotch before dinner and Cuban cigar after dinner (two habits he has sternly advised me to avoid when I'm older). Come to think of it, Lena — who despises cigar smoke and doesn't touch liquor — may put her foot down *if* they marry, she and Gramps. "If" is Lena's word, not "when." She likes to keep Gramps in suspense, or what she calls tenterhooks. Meanwhile, to add to the suspense, she hasn't given up her house in the Beaches down in Toronto.

I won't pretend that there's a happy ending as far as my grandfather and my father are concerned. I understand that they may find themselves thrown together at my fourteenth birthday party, which comes up in a few weeks, and I expect that a meeting of the two will resemble the collision of the Titanic and the iceberg. On the bright side, Mom has promised to order a pineapple-cream birthday cake, which may prevent our family celebration from sinking.

As for me, well, among the lessons I learned this summer is this: Lawyers are all alike. They make you pay for everything they do for you. Nothing is free.

After our release from the cell, and the withdrawal of the charge against me, Grandfather informed me that I owed him a great deal of money for the trouble he'd gone to in my defence.

"Wait a minute," I protested. "Isn't there a saying that blood is thicker than water?"

"Not where *I* come from, young fella," said Gramps.

"Then how much do I owe you?" I said with a peevish sneer.

"More than you can ever hope to repay," Grandfather replied.

"Okay," I said, without much enthusiasm, "I'll send you so much every week out of my allowance, if that's the way you feel."

Gramps shook his head fiercely. "Unh-unh," he said, "that's not good enough. You'll have to *work* off your debt."

"How am I supposed to do that?"

"You'll see."

"*What* will I see?"

The answer to that question turns out to be yet another of those strange turns of events. It seems I will be spending next summer up at Port Sanford, living at my grandfather's (with Lena in charge of the house, I hope, and Agnes Trimble in charge of the office).

My job will be to re-organize Grandfather's chaotic library, run messages, serve court documents, look up titles to people's properties at the land registry office, answer the phone when Agnes is on lunch or too busy to do it herself, carry Gramps' briefcase when it's too heavy for him on court days, help to keep his files in order and sneak his Cuban cigars to him so he can smoke them in the municipal park where Lena can't see.

By the way, I almost forgot to mention Hollis Burden. What happened to the man in the little black Jeep?

Here's what has happened: The very afternoon that Chief Harley Davidson brought Gramps and Josh and me back to Port Sanford, Hollis presented himself at the doorstep of the Medley brothers and their sister Priscilla Cranbrooke. The conversation went something like this, I'm told:

HAROLD MEDLEY: "Hollis? What're *you* doing here?"

BURDEN: "I guess you've heard — "

MEDLEY: "Heard what? — "

BURDEN: "That old Ira Lamport and his daughter's kid and that dog are back in town. Matter of fact, they're in front of the magistrate at this very moment."

MEDLEY: "So? What's that got to do with you, Hollis? We heard it was Chief Davidson brought'em back here, not you."

BURDEN: "Maybe. But the only reason Davidson found them was because he was hunting for *me*. It's *me* that's responsible for bringing those three back here, not Harley. If I hadn't gone after them, Davidson wouldn't've gone after me. Simple as that. So that means I'm entitled to that reward we talked about, Mr. Medley."

MEDLEY: "Sorry to disappoint you, Hollis, but my brother and sister and I don't agree with you. Now, if you'll kindly excuse us, we've a lot of business to attend to …"

The next doorstep Hollis Burden presented himself at was the doorstep of Ira Lamport. I was a witness, and this particular conversation went as follows:

GRAMPS: "Burden! What th'devil are *you* doing here?"

BURDEN: "I need a lawyer … a good one … one that'll beat the pants off the Medleys and their sister. They owe me money and I mean to collect every red cent of it. I want you to take my case, Lamport. I want you to sue them in court until they got nothing left but their underwear."

GRAMPS: "What makes you think they owe you money, Hollis?"

BURDEN: "They promised me a reward if I brought you back here to Port Sanford."

GRAMPS: "But Hollis, the fact is, it was Harley Davidson who fetched us back, not you."

BURDEN: "Don't you get it, Ira? Davidson found you because it was really *me* he was chasing after. Him and me have always been at each other over one thing or another."

GRAMPS (beginning to look intrigued): "Maybe you've got a point, Hollis, I mean legally. You must have a contract with the Medley bunch. Let me take a look at it."

BURDEN: "Ain't got a contract. I mean, I got a contract, but it was a handshake, not in writing."

GRAMPS: "Hollis, you've been around the law long enough to know that an unwritten contract isn't worth the paper it's not written on."

BURDEN: "Now look here, Ira, I didn't come here to listen to a sermon from the Old Stickler about stuff that isn't spelled out in writing. You said a minute ago I've got a point legally."

GRAMPS: "I said *maybe*, or didn't you hear me right?"

BURDEN: "Maybe's better'n nothing. It means I at least got a foot in the door."

GRAMPS: "Yeah, well don't let it go to your head, Hollis. You've had that foot in a lot of doors, often where your foot doesn't belong."

BURDEN: "I'm not asking for me and you to become bosom pals, Ira. All I'm asking is, do I have a case against them three and, if I do, then will you take it?"

Grandfather took his time before replying, playing hard to get and enjoying the sight of Hollis Burden, hat in hand, getting ready to grovel if necessary. But I could tell that the prospect of suing Rebecca O'Hearn's nephews and niece had already whetted my grandfather's lawyerly appetite. Looking intrigued again, he said, "Y'know, Hollis, sometimes even if a contract isn't in writing, you can force people to stick to their promise. You've got to prove to the judge that you went ahead and started to live up to your end of the bargain on the strength of their promise."

"That's all I needed to hear," Burden said, his face taking on a sharp look, like a hound getting hold of a scent. "I'm hiring you as my lawyer, that is, if you'll agree to take my case."

Gramps looked away. His eyes seemed to be focused on a tree down at the end of the driveway, as if there was an answer pinned to the trunk. After a pause, "We'll see, Hollis," was all he said.

"I'm asking you real nicely, Mr. Lamport."

"I said we'll see, Hollis."

Burden said, "Meantime, what I just told you ... about the Medleys and that sister of theirs ... that's in confidence, right? I mean, strictly between you and I?"

"That's bad English," Gramps huffed. "The proper expression is 'between you and *me*.'"

With that, Gramps turned and marched into the house and straight to his office, where he belonged.

# **Afterword**

S o here I am, almost a full year after the events I've just described, airing out my old beat-up duffel bag, getting ready to stuff it with clothes my mother says should have been thrown out ages ago (like baggy pants and saggy sweatshirts and sneakers that smell like a gymnasium). And, oh yes, this time I'm also taking a suit with me, the kind of thing you wear to church. Imagine, a suit! Gramps insists that if I'm going to work in his law office, I have to look — as he put it — at least *half*-human.

Mom's off in a few days to some place in South America I've never heard of, something about a revolution that she doesn't want to miss. We'll probably read her reports in the newspapers in a week or two. My father predicts that highway traffic this summer will exceed last summer's by at least ten percent, which means he'll be busier than ever patching up accident victims.

On my night table there's a bus ticket for Port Sanford, a one-way ticket by the way, because Gramps and Lena will probably drive me back home to Toronto at the end of August (in what I hope and pray will be a *new* car). Rumour has it that my grandfather actually sprang for some fresh paint and wallpaper in the house, including the room I'll be occupying.

Things are looking up for Josh, too. Gramps has set Josh up in a wicker basket large enough to accommodate a Great Dane, and why not? That six-pound Chihuahua still seems larger than life.

Miss Trimble has miraculously cleared a bit of space in Gramps' office just large enough to set up a folding card table, which will serve as my desk for the summer months.

And here's one more miracle … well, sort of a miracle: Hollis Burden's case against the Medleys and their sister Priscilla is due to come before the court early in July. In case you're wondering, Gramps says lawsuits take more time than most people appreciate. With the speed of a glacier, is the way he describes it. I still can't believe that my grandfather has become the legal champion of Hollis Burden, of all people. Talk about weird!

But, come to think of it, so much happened that I wouldn't have imagined in my wildest dreams. And the way I see the days that lie ahead — I mean, returning to Port Sanford, living under the same roof again with Stickler and his wife (I forgot to mention that Gramps and Lena were married last New Year's Day) and bumping into the likes of Chief Harley Davidson and Magistrate McEwen while trying at the same time to avoid Mrs. Bjorklund — well, as I said at the outset, the future is always scary.

## ABOUT THE AUTHOR

Morley Torgov is the author of *A Good Place to Come From*, made into a CBC mini-series and three plays for stage by Israel Horovitz, playing on and off Broadway in the mid-1980s to critical and popular acclaim and elsewhere in the USA and Canada to this day. This title was also a CLA and Book of the Month Club selection. He is also the author of *The Abramsky Variations, The Outside Chance*  *of Maximilian Glick, St. Farb's Day* and *The War to End All Wars*. He has written plays for CBC radio and television and his work has been adapted to the stage. He has twice won the Leacock Medal for Humour. Torgov received a degree from the University of Toronto, an honourary D. Litt from Laurentian University, and has written numerous articles for the *Globe and Mail, Toronto Star, Montreal Gazette, New York Times Sunday Magazine* and other periodicals. His essays have appeared in *Family Portraits* and *Beyond Imagination*. Torgov is currently at work on a detective novel and a series of children's books. He lives in Toronto where he practises law.

OTHER RAINCOAST FICTION
FOR YOUNG ADULTS AND TEENS: